WHEN JUSTICE STRIKES

Jed O'Dell, a young cowboy, prevents the rape of a young girl, but nearly gets himself killed. The girl's mother swears God has appointed him the Avenger of Blood. Now he must bring the man to justice. Jed doggedly sticks to a quest that leads to a showdown at one of Wyoming's famous hog ranches, and an encounter with one of Wyoming's most famous gunfighters. Then, within sight of his quarry, he is caught in a sudden blizzard and stares death in the face.

Books by Billy Hall
in the Linford Western Library:

KID HAILER
CLEAR CREEK JUSTICE
THE TEN SLEEP MURDERS
KING CANYON HIDEOUT
MONTANA RESCUE
CAMBDEN'S CROSSING

BILLY HALL

WHEN JUSTICE STRIKES

Complete and Unabridged

LINFORD
Leicester

First published in Great Britain in 2000 by
Robert Hale Limited
London

First Linford Edition
published 2001
by arrangement with
Robert Hale Limited
London

The moral right of the author
has been asserted

British Library CIP Data

Hall, Billy
    When justice strikes.—Large print ed.—
    Linford western library
    1. Western stories
    2. Large type books
    I. Title
    823.9′14 [F]

    ISBN 0–7089–4588–0

Published by
F. A. Thorpe (Publishing)
Anstey, Leicestershire

Set by Words & Graphics Ltd.
Anstey, Leicestershire
Printed and bound in Great Britain by
T. J. International Ltd., Padstow, Cornwall

This book is printed on acid-free paper

1

His face was ashen. He swallowed twice. His profusely sweating hand made the handle of his pistol slick, slipping and sliding in his grip. He shifted the heavy Colt .45 to his left hand. The planks of the cow shed were rough against his face. He pushed himself away from it, but stayed well clear of the corner. Wiping his hand on his pants leg, he moved the gun back to his right hand.

The gun still slipped. Shaking his head, he started to lay the gun on the ground. He shook his head again, then placed the gun in its holster. He leaned back against the vertical slabs of the shed. His hands trembled slightly as he untied his neckerchief and used it to wipe the sweat from his hands. He drew the gun again and wiped the sweat from it as well. He gripped the gun and moved it back and forth. He nodded his satisfaction: it no longer felt too slick to hold.

He jammed the neckerchief into his pocket and leaned his head back against the side of the shed. He took a deep breath, gathering himself, and poked his head around the corner. Instantly, splinters flew from the wood, inches from his face.

He ducked back with a stifled curse, he lost his balance and fell backward. Muttering something unintelligible, he scrambled back to his feet, gritting his teeth so hard the muscles bunched at the corners of his jaws. Cringing, his eyes squinted almost shut, he thrust his gun around the corner and fired blindly twice.

He jerked his arm back, took another deep breath, then squatted down and took the neckerchief from his pocket, using it to mop the sweat from his forehead. A sudden sound of hoofbeats clattered in the still air. He jumped to his feet and jammed the neckerchief back into his pocket, then peered carefully around the corner of the wood shed again. Nothing happened.

His knees wobbled noticeably as he stepped into the open. A slowly spreading line of dust drifted lazily in the still air. His eyes followed the trail of that narrow dust cloud toward the neck of timber that jutted into the dry valley. The fleeing horseman was already out of sight.

A timid voice spoke at his elbow. 'Is . . . is he gone?'

Jed O'Dell turned slowly. He faced the young girl. Her dress was torn in several places; one eye was swollen nearly shut, the dark skin encircling it rapidly turning purple. A trickle of blood ran from the corner of her mouth. She held the tattered dress across herself to protect the battered shreds of her modesty. The effort was not wholly successful. In spite of her youth, she had a striking figure.

Jed's lips compressed to a thin line. It took a supreme effort to keep forcing his eyes up to the girl's face. His eyes seemed to have a mind of their own: they kept dropping to that ill-concealed figure. He swallowed hard.

'He's gone,' he said. 'He lit out thataway.'

The girl's dark eyes darted toward the distant tree-line, then back to Jed. She appeared almost calm, except that those eyes were open too widely and the pupils were dilated. They, too, seemed to have a mind of their own as they kept that darting dance from Jed's face to the distant trees. Back and forth they darted. Back and forth.

She spoke again, her voice a shade too shrill. 'Will he come back? He will, won't he? He'll wait till you're gone, then he'll come back after me again.'

Jed shook his head. 'I don't think so. No, I'm sure not, in fact. No, he won't come back.'

'Yes he will. He will. I know he will. He wants to hurt me. He wants to . . . to . . . to r-r-ra — to use me. He'll wait till I'm all alone here, and then he'll come back.'

Jed felt cornered. He looked around, trying to see somebody else. There must be someone else around the place! The girl continued to prattle frantically.

He interrupted the torrent of her fear. 'Hey! You gotta stop that there talk. Where's your ma, child?'

His tone stopped the torrent of words, but evoked no reply. The question was answered instead by a woman running frantically around the corner of the rude house.

'Allie! Allie! Are you all right? I heard gunshots. I was clear down to the crick. Oh! Oh, Allie, what happened to you?'

Her eyes darted to Jed. Her posture changed from fear to anger. She leaned forward, jabbing a finger at Jed. 'Who are you? What have you done to my Allie?'

Jed held up both hands, palms toward the rushing woman. 'It wasn't me! She's OK, ma'am. They was a man tried to ... to, uh, have 'is way with her. I just rode up on 'em. I run 'im off.

She's beat up some, but I think she's OK.'

The woman looked back and forth from Jed to Allie. Her hands twisted in the folds of her dress. Time itself seemed to hang suspended as she digested the information. Then Allie's face dissolved. With a plaintive wail, she dropped the tatters of her dress and reached toward her mother. The dress fell away from her young body, as mother and daughter lunged into each other's arms. Jed looked away hurriedly.

When he thought it was safe, he glanced furtively out the corner of his eye. He sighed loudly. There was no response. He cleared his throat. They continued to ignore him. He turned back to face the pair. Allie was sobbing uncontrollably into her mother's shoulder. Her mother was crooning softly to her, her face buried in the girl's hair.

Jed cleared his throat yet again. 'Uh, ma'am, is your husband close by somewheres?'

The woman's face rose from her

daughter's hair. She looked at him sharply. A shudder ran through her. She ignored Jed's question. She pushed Allie to arm's length, but keeping a hand on each of the girl's shoulders. She looked directly into the girl's teary eyes and spoke sternly.

'Tell me what happened, Allie,' she said. 'You forget there's anybody here 'cept just you an' me. You tell me everything. You hear me? Tell it all.'

Allie struggled to stifle her sobs. She wiped her face with the sleeve of her tattered dress. Suddenly remembering Jed's presence, she jerked up the dress in front of herself again.

Jed was so busy studying the girl's face he forgot to be embarrassed. Even the tears and the recent beating couldn't conceal her beauty. Couldn't be more'n fifteen, he thought. Same as Bertie was. An' just as much a woman.

Allie took a deep, ragged breath. She tried valiantly to keep the tremor from her voice. 'I was bringin' in a armload o' wood, like you tol' me to,' she said

7

softly. 'A man done rode up an' asked me where you was. I tol' him you was down by the crick, pickin' blackberries. He asked me where my pa was. I tol' 'im Pa was gone off to town.'

'You shouldn't never tell some stranger that!' her mother interrupted. 'I tol' you that a hunert times! You tell 'im your pa's right behind the house, or in the barn. Then you got a chance to get away or hide or get a gun or somethin', if'n he turns out to be a bad sort. They's all kinds o' bad sorts runnin' round, ever since the war. I keep tellin' you that. If'n your pa'd ever get a real door put on, you could maybe bar it, in a time like that.'

The girl hung her head and studied the ground. Her mother poked her with the dirty fingernail of a blackberry-stained hand. 'Well, go on.'

Allie took a deep breath and continued. 'Well, then he asked me for a drink. I went in an' got 'im a dipper o' water outa the bucket. When I come out with it he drunk it. Then he reached out and grabbed me. He said he'd been on the trail without no woman for too long. He said I was real purty, an' he tried to kiss me. I up an' slapped him, just as hard as I could. It musta hurt, too, cuz he hollered real loud. Then he started cussin' me somethin' awful, and hittin' me and tearin' at my dress, and he throwed me on the ground and started puttin' his hands all over on me and laughin' a plumb awful laugh, and he said he was gonna . . . gonna . . . oh, Mommaaa!'

She reached for her mother again, and clung to her, sobbing for several minutes. When her sobs subsided, her mother pushed her away again. Neither made any effort to lift the tatters of the dress that hung from Allie's waist. Jed looked off across the valley. He shifted his feet and cleared his throat yet again. They both ignored his presence and his discomfort completely.

'Tell me the rest of it, Allie. Git it all out.'

Allie made another valiant attempt to

control the ragged emotion in her breath. 'That's all there's to tell, Momma,' she sobbed. 'That was when this here man come ridin' up. He hollered, 'Hey! What d'ya think you're doin',' or somethin' like that. The guy jumped offa me, and jerked out his gun an' shot at 'im, but he didn't hit 'im none, I guess. Then he run out behind, chasin' after 'is horse. I run in the house, an' I heard 'em shootin'. Then I heard a horse runnin' off, so I come back outside, and the guy was gone. Oh, Momma, he hurt me. He hit me awful hard.'

She would have collapsed into tears again, but her mother would have none of it. 'That's tears enough. It's no use to cry any more about it. Go in the house and change your clothes,' she said gently. 'You're all right. You were lucky. The Good Lord was watchin' out fer ya. You just have a few bruises. This man has saved you from being hurt any worse. Now you go on in the house.'

Jed stood in silence until the girl

disappeared past the hanging buffalo hide that served as a door. Then he looked into the steely eyes of the woman.

'You let him get away,' she accused abruptly. 'He tried to rape my daughter, and you let him just up an' ride away.'

Jed's jaw dropped. 'Ma'am, I stopped him from what he was fixin' to do. I run 'im off. I ain't no gunfighter; I'm just a cowboy. I done everythin' I could.'

'Well, it wasn't enough. You let him get away. Now you have to find him, you know. It's your duty.'

'What?'

'You have to pursue him. You have to find him, to capture him. You have to bring him to justice, or kill him.'

'But, ma'am! I ain't no lawman; I ain't no gunfighter, neither. I couldn't stand up to the likes o' him for ten seconds. Ma'am, you ought've seen the way he drawed that gun o' his. He jumped offa that there little ol' girl o' yours, and whirled, and his gun was already in his hand, an' I didn't even see 'im draw it. He's powerful fast. He snapped off a shot at me, with his pants half off and your girl kickin' at 'im, and it was so close I felt it buzzin' past my ear!'

'All the more reason he must be brought to justice,' the woman said firmly. 'He is obviously a man who relies on his gun and who takes whatever he wants from whomever he runs across. There are scarcely any lawmen in this country to stop such men, so the duty falls to any decent and honourable man who encounters such a one. You are a decent and honourable man, are you not?'

Jed felt his face flush. 'Yes, ma'am. I am. But — '

She did not allow him to finish. 'And do you consider yourself a Christian?'

'Well, sure. Yeah. I been brought up Christian.'

'Then you may consider yourself God's chosen instrument to exact justice and to protect other young ladies like my daughter from falling into

12

his clutches. You must pursue him, find him, and bring him to justice. You can track, can't you?'

Jed shifted his feet uncomfortably. 'Well, yes, ma'am, I could do that. I'm a first-rate tracker, but I ain't no gunman at all. I even take two or three shots to get a deer. If I even get 'im.'

'God will provide for your deficiencies,' she interrupted. 'I appoint you the Avenger of Blood, and the protector of my daughter's honour.'

'Avenger of Blood?'

'Avenger of Blood,' she repeated. 'You have read about that in the Good Book, haven't you?'

'Uh, well, no, ma'am. That is, I cain't read none. I ain't never had no schoolin'.'

'Well, you may take my word for it. It's in there. Thus saith the Lord. I know you're not the kind of man to go against God, or to go against what's written in the Good Book. You wouldn't refuse to obey God, would you, young man?'

'Oh, no, ma'am. I wouldn't wanta do that.'

'Then it's settled. You may water your horse. I will pack some provisions for your trip. Then you must go, before he gets any further ahead of you.'

She wheeled without waiting for any further answer and disappeared into the house. Jed stared in disbelief after her. 'She never even thanked me!' he told his horse. 'Now she thinks she can 'appoint' me to go chasin' that, that, who knows what he is?'

He led his horse to the water tank by the crude corral. The horse tossed her head several times to push the green coating on the water aside. Then she began to drink the tepid water thirstily.

As the horse buried her nose in the mossy water, Jed leaned on the top rail. 'Still an' all,' he muttered, 'if I don't at least try to stop 'im, how many more is he goin' to do that to? What'll happen if someone don't ride along, next time? What if she's right. If'n God really says that there, an' I don't do it, they ain't no tellin' what'll happen to me! Now why'd I have to go an' be the one that rode up?'

His horse lifted her nose from the water. She shook her head, splattering Jed with spray from her nose and face, making the bit jingle softly.

The woman's voice interrupted his reverie. 'You'd be wantin' a drink of water, too?'

He turned and accepted the dipper of water from the woman's hand. He studied her over the rim of the dipper as he drank. Too many years of too hard work and too much Wyoming sun had taken a toll on the face that must once have been as soft and beautiful as her daughter's. Now it more closely resembled the checks and lines of old leather. Husks of dead dreams and the ghosts of old sorrows moved in the shadows behind her dark eyes.

'You look a lot like my mother,' he said softly.

The harsh lines of her face softened

slightly. 'Where is your mother?' she asked.

Against his will, Jed's mind went back. He saw again the bodies of his mother and sister, lying naked and bloated in the sun. He saw the bullet-riddled body of his father in the door of the barn. 'They're dead,' he said simply.

'I'm sorry,' the woman offered. 'Indians?'

He shook his head. 'Never knew who,' he said. 'Found 'em one day. I was just a-comin' home to visit. They was all three dead. Out in the yard. Ma an' Bertie'd been raped; Pa was shot to pieces: he didn't even have a gun on 'im.'

Sympathy further softened the harsh lines of the woman's face. Her voice was noticeably softer. 'Did you find the ones who did it?'

He felt his face redden with the shame that lay always just beneath the surface of his mind. He just shook his head.

16

Her face hardened again perceptibly, 'Did you try? You did try, didn't you?'

He nodded, wordlessly. He had tried. He had tried his best. He felt again the grim determination to become a gunman, so he could hunt down and destroy the men who had committed the heinous crime. He remembered the beginning of his shame that came with the lack of ability the effort had revealed. He could never get the hang of drawing and shooting quickly and had nearly shot his own foot several times, trying.

Even now, he couldn't even hit his target fully half the time. He wore a .45. He carried a .30/.30 carbine in his saddle. He could use them, when he had to. He just wasn't very good.

He wasn't much of a detective, either. All of his very best efforts hadn't revealed the identity of the men who had ravished and destroyed his family. Time had slowly dulled the zeal for vengeance that had driven him relentlessly for more than a year. In the intervening five years he had settled for being a first-rate cowhand, wherever he could hire on. The memory of his family as he had last seen them had never left him, however. A persistent voice in the centre of his soul still cried for vengeance, for justice.

He shook his head. 'Never even found out who it was.'

Her face took on a calculating look. 'Well maybe the Good Lord's giving you a second chance. Maybe that's why you happened along today. You never know. It could have even been one of the same men.'

Jed's head jerked up. His mind raced. Was it possible this was one of the same men? No! That was ridiculous! The odds against that were unimaginable. But even so, was this his chance to redeem himself for not avenging his own family?

'Here's a packet of food and things. I'd invite you in to eat, but I'm sure you want to get started afore that trail gets cold.'

'He turned to face the granite face of Allie's mother. He thought of telling her simply that following the man could only result in his own death. A deep chill in his stomach assured him that was surely true. Instead he simply said, 'Thank you, ma'am.'

He stepped into the saddle. He took the carefully wrapped package of provisions from her hands. 'That's our last side of bacon,' she said. Her voice suddenly sounded suspiciously brusque. 'You'll be needin' strength to stay on the trail. My husband will be back from town tomorrow. We'll be asking Providence to help you do what's got to be done.'

She turned without waiting for a reply and disappeared again into the house. Jed lifted the reins and sent his horse to follow the trail of his destiny. Or his death.

2

Jed jerked his horse to a standstill. He stood in the stirrups, shading his eyes with his hand, as he squinted against the sun.

A horse burst from the trees a hundred yards ahead. It was running toward him, but it was running strangely. Then he saw the reason: the horse was running while sidling away from a bouncing, yelling bundle at its left side. A rider had been thrown and his foot had slipped through the stirrup, instead of sliding free. Now the foot was hung up on the opposite side of the stirrup.

The rider's vest was pulled over his head and his hands flopped helplessly. He kept trying to double his body enough to reach the foot, grab the stirrup strap and pull himself up enough to free the entangled foot. Each time he almost reached it, the horse made an extra bound, snapping him back. His head and his shoulders were bouncing on rocks, brush and ground. Each effort he made was more feeble than the last.

Jed jerked loose the strap holding his lariat. He jabbed the spurs to his horse's sides. 'C'mon Rosie,' he called to her. 'Go get 'im.'

The horse responded without hesitation, her ears flattened back, her head thrust forward and down. She bunched her back legs under her and hinged forward. In three jumps she was in full stride. She ran, nose outstretched, her belly nearly touching the ground at the extreme of each stretch.

Jed shook out a loop using three or four coils of his lariat. He leaned forward and slightly to the right. He began to whirl the loop over his head.

The horse took up a line just to the left of the fleeing mount, gaining on it swiftly. As they closed on the frightened animal, Jed loosed his rope with a mighty heave. The loop reached out ahead of them, settling neatly over the outstretched head of the runaway.

As soon as the loop began its descent, Jed's horse braced her front feet. She spread her feet apart, crouching her hind quarters low to the ground, sliding in the grass, kicking up sod and dust. The rope tightened just as the loop closed over the horse's neck. The horse recognized it was caught at the same time, and set its own feet. It was only that quick recognition that kept it from being jerked from its feet by the sudden tether.

By the time both animals were stopped, Jed had leaped to the ground. He hit the earth running, one hand on the taut lariat for balance. His horse kept backing just enough to keep that rope tight, so it could not be dislodged.

The caught runaway wheeled around, facing the pair who had captured it. Its ears, too, were laid back, its eyes rolling wildly; snorting and squealing its fear and frustration.

Jed ignored the horse. He ran to the left stirrup and grabbed the leg of the downed rider. He jerked up the stirrup and slipped the foot through it, freeing the snagged limb of the hapless rider.

As the foot came free, the man's mount sidled away. Jed's horse kept the rope taut, preventing it from fleeing. Jed and the rider he had rescued were left in a cleared area, out of danger of dancing hooves.

Jed looked at the rider, then quickly pulled his eyes away. The rider's shirt had followed the vest in being dragged up over the head. As he started to pull them down from the face, to assess the amount of damage done, he could not fail to notice the rider was most certainly not a man. He hesitated only an instant. As gently as possible, he gathered the ends of the shirt tail and pulled them downward, beneath the motionless rider's back. Then he pulled the front of the shirt tails down, covering her. Then he did the same with the vest, allowing him to see her face for the first time.

Flaming red hair cascaded outward, framing a youthful face as though it were the centre of a great sunburst of colour. Her nose was slightly large, with a prominent hooked bridge; her eyes were widely spaced, and closed; her mouth was small, and sagged open slightly. She neither moved nor made any sound.

Jed swallowed hard. He started to lay his ear on her chest to listen for a heartbeat, then thought better of it. He picked up her hand and shook it lightly.

'You OK, ma'am?' he asked. 'Can you hear me?'

There was no answer. He looked around, There was no sign of any other person in any direction. He swallowed again. He took off his hat and he laid it on the ground, then laid his head on her chest to listen for a heartbeat. He was instantly gratified to hear a strong, steady pulse. He also heard clearly the sound of slow, steady breathing.

'Well, you're alive,' he told the

unresponsive girl. 'Let's see if we can figure out how bad you're hurt.'

He gently picked up the girl's head. He ran an exploring hand across the back of her skull. 'Wow! There's how come you're out cold,' he said. 'You got a bump the size of a small pine cone back there.'

The skin did not appear broken and there was no blood. He laid her head back down gently, picked up each arm in turn, feeling up and down the length of each. 'Don't seem to have neither arm busted,' he said.

He examined each of her legs as best he could. The ankle of the foot that had been hung up was swollen, but did not appear broken.

She moaned. He lifted her head and shifted her weight so her head was in the crook of his arm. He tried to hold her so she would not move and thrash around as she came to.

Her eyes opened. A glaze slowly melted from the pupils, as light slowly floods the earth at sunrise. She jerked away from him abruptly. 'Don't touch me!' she yelled.

She leaped to her feet, then wobbled sideways. She would have fallen if he had not caught her. 'Hey, it's all right,' Jed said, as soothingly as he could. 'You got hung up in a stirrup. I spotted you, an' roped your horse. You're OK. You just got a knock on the head.'

She sagged against him, her knees buckling weakly. Her head lolled into that crook of his arm again, her eyes bearing the look of a trapped animal. She started to push away from him, then her eyes focused on him for the first time. A look of confusion passed across them. She hesitated, with a hand against his chest, her head still resting against the curl of his arm. 'You're . . . you're not him. You . . . '

She left the sentence hang there unfinished. Her eyes darted around and came back to rest on Jed's face. 'What happened?'

Jed explained again. 'You got throwed, looked like. Your horse done

26

come a-bustin' outa the trees with you a-floppin' and bouncin' along, all hung up in the stirrup. I seed what was goin' on, and me'n ol' Rosie here chased you down an' roped your horse to stop 'im. I 'spect maybe your head bounced off'n a rock somewheres along there.'

She relaxed against him, trusting his arm for support. He was only too happy to provide it. 'My head hurts,' she said simply.

'You got a right big goose egg back there, right enough,' he said. 'It ain't bleedin' or nothin', though. I didn't find no busted bones or nothin' neither. I reckon you're just right lucky.'

'How long was I out?'

'Oh, ten, fifteen minutes, I 'spect. What in tarnation you doin' ridin' a spooky horse with them moccasins, 'stead o' boots? Don't you know you can get hung up thataway?'

She sighed heavily. A shudder passed through her body. 'Buck's usually not spooky. I ride him with my moccasins on all the time. I don't like boots:

they're hot and heavy, and they make so much noise if I want to get off and sneak up where I can watch deer or wild turkeys or something.'

'What spooked 'im?'

She shuddered again and hesitated quite a while before answering. Testing the strength of her legs to hold her, she pushed away from him and walked a few steps growing steadier with each step. 'I think I'm OK. I'm not as dizzy now.'

'What spooked your horse?' he asked again.

She looked at the distant line of trees and shuddered again. She looked back at Jed a long moment before answering. 'There was a man. I don't know him. I've never seen him before. I was sitting under a tree watching a coyote trying to take a dead jack-rabbit away from an eagle. The rabbit was too big for the eagle to carry it and fly more than just a little ways. Then the coyote would catch up, and the eagle would fly a little further. It was really fun to watch.

'Then I looked around and this man was standing there staring at me. I didn't even hear him ride up. He was halfway between me and his horse, and he was just watching me. I said, 'Hello', or something, I don't remember. He just walked up to me, real fast, and grabbed me. He said, 'Well, hello, sweetie', or something like that, and tried to kiss me.'

She shuddered again. 'What'd you do?' Jed asked.

'I slipped out of his arms and kicked him, just as hard as I could, and ran. I got to my horse and jumped on and told him to run for all he was worth. He did, too. Buck can run really fast.'

'So how'd you get throwed?'

Her voice echoed her confusion and pain. 'I don't know. I thought we'd gotten clear away from him, and we were almost to the end of that stretch of timber, then Buck saw something. He shied really hard. He just jumped straight sideways. I lost my balance. Then whatever it was scared him, and he started running. It might have been a bear. Then when I got hung up in the stirrup, it scared him even more, and he ran away with me.'

Jed digested the information slowly. 'Who was the man?'

She shook her head, then obviously wished she hadn't done so. She held it with both hands a moment before she answered. 'I don't know,' she said. 'I never saw him before.'

'Was he big?'

She nodded her head, slowly and carefully, this time. 'He was really big, and had a really big black beard. He was dirty and smelled awful. His teeth, when he grinned at me, were all brown and a couple of them were broken. That's really all I saw. I just wanted to get away from him.'

Jed nodded. 'You're plumb lucky you did,' he said. 'I been trackin' 'im fer a day an' a half. He tried to rape another girl up yonder along the Little Thunder.'

She gasped. Her hands moved

unconsciously to her leather vest, pulling it together across her chest and gripping it with both hands. 'Are you a marshal or something?'

'Uh, no, ma'am. I ain't nothin' special at all. I just happened along, that time, and I was given the job o' tryin' to track 'im down. He's a bad 'un.'

She looked at him for a long moment. 'I don't think I said, thank you,' she said, finally. 'You saved my life.'

Jed felt suddenly awkward and at a loss for words. 'Aw, I didn't do nothin' nobody else wouldn'ta done. I just happened to be the one what spotted you.'

'But you did save my life. Thank you.'

'You live round here?'

'My husband and I have our homestead on Porcupine Creek, just above where it joins Lazy Fork. My name is Nancy Walters. My husband is Harvey. I call him Curly, because he has this really cute curl of hair that comes up off of his shirt collar.'

She gave him a sidelong glance as though they were co-conspirators in some amusing piece of knowledge. A smile played at the corners of her mouth as she continued, 'Nobody else calls him that, though. That's just my own name for him. And he's got this other cute curl that . . . ' She giggled unexpectedly. 'Well, never mind. Anyway, sometimes he works on Sundays, but I don't like to, so sometimes I go for a ride. We're really lucky. We have a nice starter herd and some good horses, and a better homestead than most people. My parents helped us, and we even have a real house with glass windows! You should see it. We're going to build a real ranch out of it. I homesteaded another quarter right beside Harvey's, so we'll own a half-section of water from both cricks. Oh, I'm sorry. I think maybe I'm running off at the mouth again. I talk too much when I get excited or scared, and I was really scared. My head really,

really hurts. I really wish I was just home.'

'You want me to help you home?'

'Oh, I can . . . I mean . . . would you do that? I've never been afraid to ride by myself in my life, but I'm afraid.'

'I'd be plumb happy to see you home. I'll get my rope off'n your horse an' you lead the way.'

They rode for nearly an hour. At the outset, Nancy continued the pattern of chatter. Her prattle was too bubbly, too happy for the circumstances. Jed tried to make sense of it, but it became increasingly difficult to follow any train of thought. Then her voice trailed off, and she only mumbled. The mumbles gave way to silence. Then she began to sway noticeably in the saddle. 'You OK, ma'am?' Jed asked.

There was no answer. Jed rode up close beside her and grabbed her arm. She appeared not to notice. 'You OK, ma'am?' he asked again.

She swayed against him, and he caught her, holding her upright in the saddle. 'Here, you best slide over here with me, so's I can hold you from fallin' off again,' he said.

Jed stopped his horse. Nancy's horse stopped as well. He dropped a loop of his lariat over the head of Nancy's horse and took a dally on his own saddle horn, to lead the animal. He knotted the reins and hooked them over the saddle horn, where they could not fall off and drag, then he slid over the cantle of his own saddle, sitting right against the back of its seat. He lifted Nancy from her horse on to his own. He was surprised at how light she was.

He reached around her and lifted the reins of his horse. She leaned back against him, only semiconscious at best. 'I sure hope I can find their place from what description she done give me in all that there chatterin' she was doin',' he said. 'That knock on the head just went an' knocked her plumb goofy.'

He reflected on the thought a moment. 'I don't reckon she's no goofier'n I am, though, settin' off on a fool thing like trackin' that guy. Well, leastways I done saved one life by a-doin' it, and a woman at that. Not to mention a right purty one. Now I wonder if'n someone's gonna save my skin if'n I catch up with that guy.'

It was, in fact, an appropriate thing to wonder.

3

'Hold it right there! Get your hands off my wife. Put your hands in the air, quick, or I'll blow you clear out of the saddle.'

Jed reined his horse to a stop. He turned his head slowly, and found himself looking directly down the barrel of a .50 Sharps rifle. He swallowed hard.

'Uh, I, uh, I can't. I can't let loose. She'll fall, don't you know?'

'Take your hands off my wife and throw up your hands like I told you, or I'll blow your head clear off your shoulders.'

Anger began to overcome the rush of terror and surprise in Jed. 'Are you Harvey Walters?'

'I'm Harvey Walters, and that woman you're tryin' to kidnap is my wife, and you picked on the wrong one. You're a dead man, mister. Now put up your hands. I'd just as soon shoot you as try to take you to the sheriff for hangin', so you better do what I say.'

'It ain't like that there at all. I ain't tryin' to kidnap your wife. I saved her life.'

'Stop jawin' and get your hands up.'

The anger was clearly in control, now. He ignored the rifle and glared at its owner across the top of its barrel. 'No,' Jed replied sharply.

'No? What do you mean, no?'

'No. I ain't turnin' loose, and I ain't puttin' my hands up. An' you can put that rifle down an' try usin' your head. Either that or go ahead an' shoot, an' kill your wife in the process.'

The rifle lowered, almost imperceptibly 'What?'

'I said, 'Use your head'. Your wife's been hurt. She's out cold. If I let 'er loose and throw up my hands, she's gonna fall down there on the ground, and get hurt some more. I ain't none

37

too sure she can take much more gettin' hurt.'

The man hesitated. He lowered the rifle a few inches. 'Then you better tell me what's goin' on. And it better be good. Remember, I'm just about that close to blowin' you right out of the saddle.'

'How about we get your wife home first, you hotheaded idiot, then you can hear the story to your heart's content? Where's your place?'

'What?'

'I said, where's your place?'

'You're lookin' for my place?'

'Of course I'm lookin' fer your place, you danged knucklehead, cuz I'm tryin' to get your wife home. Now where is it?'

The shadows had grown grotesquely long. The sun was dangerously close to disappearing behind the Big Horn Mountains to the west. Jed's arms ached from holding the unconscious girl in the saddle in front of him. The lead rope attached to the woman's own horse rubbed and chafed across his leg, even through his chaps, and he dared not release either hand to move it to a less tender spot.

He had heard nothing from the woman except her rhythmic breathing in the past hour and a half. He had tried several times to wake her up, then given up the attempt. He would just have to hope she was still alive, and that he could find her homestead.

He had found a trickle of a stream he thought might be Lazy Fork, and had followed it downstream, riding to the east-north-east. When it merged with the slightly larger flow of Porcupine Creek he turned left, following the larger creek upstream. He knew the homestead would be much closer riding directly across country, but he didn't know its location. The only way he could be certain of finding it was to follow the streams. He had thought he must be close when he had unexpectedly found himself looking down the rifle barrel. He had no idea where the man had come from.

'Uh, it's just over the rise. You go ahead. I'll follow you. And don't forget, I'm right behind you, and I don't miss with this Sharps.'

Jed snorted and nudged the horse forward. He topped the rise and spotted a set of buildings. They matched the description she had given in the half-coherent ramblings that marked the beginning of the ride. A small house made of cut lumber stood on the crown of a small rise, with tall timber sheltering it from three sides. The fourth side, facing north-east, faced the creek and the open country beyond. A real horse barn, soundly built though also small, stood to the west of the house, right against the edge of the timber. Corrals fanned out from the barn, providing more than adequate pens to work a small herd of cattle.

'Well, she was sure right about the place,' Jed admired. 'They're built fer the long haul. They's gonna have a right smart spread in a few years, barrin' blizzards or somethin' such.'

Jed made no effort to reason with the man until they reached the house. He stopped before the front door. The man walked around him, holding the rifle at waist level, still trained on Jed. Jed's patience reached an end. 'Will you put that danged rifle down and give me a hand, now?'

The man fingered the gun nervously, clearly confused about what he should do. Jed sighed with resignation. Then he said, 'Is this here your wife?'

'Yes. That's Nancy. She's my wife. What happened?'

'Her horse done throwed 'er, and she got hung up. I roped the horse, and stopped 'im. She ain't got nothin' busted, I don't think, but she done got a whopper of a goose egg on the noggin.'

'She's alive, ain't she? She's OK, ain't she?'

'She's alive, sure 'nuff. She was a-talkin' OK, and I asked her did she want me to see 'er home, an' she said 'yeah', an' then, whilst we was a-ridin', she commenced to talkin' kinda crazy-like, an' then she quit talkin' at all. I couldn't get her to talk no more, an' I didn't want 'er fallin' off an' gettin' hurt no more, so I sorta drug 'er over on to my horse where I could hold 'er on.'

Harvey finally lowered the rifle. He lowered the hammer and stood it beside the door, leaning it against the wall. 'Well, give her here. No, don't. You help me get her in the house, and we'll see how bad she's hurt.'

Jed nodded. He swung his right foot around awkwardly to get it free of the lead rope and dropped to the ground. Then they eased Nancy over sideways, lifting her from the saddle. Harvey Walters wrapped his arms around her shoulders, holding her close to him, with her head cradled in the crook of his arm. His forehead was deeply furrowed. He appeared close to tears. Jed picked up her feet, and they carried her into the small house. Jed resisted the impulse to kick the Sharps rifle into the dirt as they walked past it.

The house was divided into three rooms. They carried her into the bedroom and laid her on the bed. Harvey stroked the side of her face. 'Can you hear me, Nance? Try to open your eyes.'

Her eyelids fluttered open. She looked at her husband uncomprehendingly for a moment, then her eyes focused. 'Hi, honey,' she said softly. Her eyes closed and she seemed to go to sleep.

Both men stood looking at her awkwardly. Finally Jed cleared his throat. 'Uh, why don't you check 'er over some, an' make sure she ain't hurt none, 'cept that knock on the head. I'll go put the horses up. That is, if'n you don't mind me a-puttin' my horse up in your barn, an' givin' 'im a bait a grub, too.'

'Oh, yeah. Sure. Yeah, why don't you do that. No, put your horse up, and I'll check Nance out an' make sure she's

OK, an' then I'll stir us up some supper. Yeah. Yeah, that's a good idea. Why don't you do that. Uh, my horse is down there in the trees, just where I jumped you. I was just ridin' out to try to find my Nancy. Would you mind goin' down there and getting him and putting him in the barn for me too?'

Jed nodded wordlessly. He fled as though he were being pursued. He took the horses to the barn. There were four stalls for horses, and only one occupied. He unsaddled Nancy's horse, put the gear away, and put hay in the stall for it. He recoiled his lariat and secured it to his saddle. Then he mounted and rode out after Harvey's horse. He found him with no difficulty, led him back to the barn, and unsaddled both animals. When he had fed them both, he hung around the barn for what seemed like an hour, waiting to give Walters time to sort things out and settle down. Twice he nearly decided to saddle his horse and ride out again. Then he thought better of it.

'If'n I did that there, an' she up an' died, I wouldn't have nobody to tell no one that I didn't do it. If'n I took off a-runnin', it'd look sure 'nuff like I did. No, I guess I'd best stick around an' hope she's OK.'

When he returned to the house, Walters was already busy cooking supper. The smell of frying potatoes and venison steaks famished Jed immediately, 'Boy, that smells good,' he said.

Harvey turned from the stove. 'Sorry I was so jumpy, out there,' he said. 'Nancy didn't come back when she should've, so I'd just saddled up to try to find her, but I didn't even know where to look. I was just plumb beside myself with worryin'.'

'She wake up yet?'

'Yeah, a little, twice. She's got the hide peeled off her back somethin' awful. I done rubbed some ointment we got on it good. And she's bruised up all over. There don't seem to be anything busted. Just that bump on the head. She said something about you savin'

45

her. Then she said something else I didn't understand. Something about a black beard.'

'She was probably tryin' to tell you 'bout that feller what latched on to 'er.'

Harvey nearly dropped the frying pan he was holding to stir the potatoes. 'What? Who? What are you talking about?'

'She got throwed runnin' away from some feller what tried to latch on to 'er. That's how she come to get hung up.'

'Somebody tried to grab my Nancy? Who?'

'I don't rightly know his name. Big man. Full beard. Bad sort. I been trackin' 'im. That there's how come I comed along. He done went an' tried to rape a little fifteen-year-old girl up yonder, along the Little Thunder Crick.'

Harvey swallowed hard. He seemed at a complete loss for words. He turned back to the stove and devoted his attention to finishing the frying of their supper. When he was finished, he piled two plates high with it, and put a lesser amount on a third plate. He crossed the kitchen wordlessly and disappeared into the bedroom. Jed could hear the murmur of voices from that room, and felt a great rush of relief that one of the voices was Nancy's.

Harvey came out and got the plate with the lesser portion and carried it into the bedroom. As he came back, Jed said, 'She's awake?'

Harvey nodded. 'She says she's got a granddaddy of a headache, and she gets dizzy if she tries to sit up too straight or move around much, but she's awake. She's gonna eat as much as she feels like in bed. I 'spect I'll be makin' her stay in bed a few days.'

'Be a good idee, I reckon.'

'Now tell me all about what happened.'

Between mouthfuls of venison and fried potatoes, Jed filled him in. He started in with his chance discovery of the attempted rape in progress. When he got to the part about the girl's mother naming him as the Avenger of Blood, Harvey nodded his head.

'That's in the Good Book, all right. I always thought it had to be a relative of the one that got killed or whatever, though.'

'It's really in there, though? There really is such a thing as an Avenger o' Blood?'

Harvey nodded his head emphatically. 'Oh, it's there, sure enough. I don't know as I could tell you chapter and verse, or anything like that, but it's there, sure's anything.'

Jed pondered the new bit of information silently. Somehow he had hoped someone would tell him the woman had made up the whole thing. Then he would be relieved of any responsibility to pursue it. Instead, he received confirmation. It was not what he wanted. Harvey waited politely for him to resume the story.

Jed finally did. 'Well, anyway, I guess I sorta accepted that, an' said I'd do it. I lit out an' commenced to trackin' 'im.

That's one thing I can do with the best of 'em. I can track real well. I was againin' on 'im purty good, too. Then I seed your wife, only I didn't know it was your wife right then, o' course. I didn't even know it was a woman. I just seed this here horse bust outa the timber a'draggin' 'is rider. So I shook out a loop an' hauled 'im in, and then that's when I figured out it was a girl.'

'Was she conscious when you got her horse stopped?'

'Nope. She didn't wake up for ten or fifteen minutes. She was a'breathin', an' her heart sounded fine. Uh, I sorta had to listen to her heart, to make sure she was alive an' all. I hope you don't mind that. It was just somethin' I sorta had to do. I wasn't tryin' to be improper, or nothin' like that there.'

Harvey nodded wordlessly, so Jed continued. 'Well, after about ten or fifteen minutes, she woked up, and got all excited fer just a minute till she seed I wasn't the feller what tried to latch on to 'er. Then she tol' me what happened.

She was sittin' under a tree, watchin' a coyote an' a eagle fightin' over a big ol' jack-rabbit, she said, and this feller just walks up an' grabs 'er and tries to commence to kissin' her. She kicked 'im and got away, and jumped on 'er horse an' run off from 'im.'

'Did you see him?'

'Naw, I didn't see nothin' of 'im at all. 'Course, I was sorta busy commencin' to try to catch that horse o' hers. Anyway, she was talkin' OK, then, only too much, sorta. Kinda runnin' on some. Then when we was ridin' back here . . . I asked her did she want me to see 'er home — '

Harvey broke in, 'You told me that.'

'Oh, yeah. Well, anyway, that's how it was.'

Harvey sighed heavily. He got up and went into the bedroom. He came out with Nancy's plate. About half the food had been eaten. 'She's asleep again, but she seems to be sleeping OK.'

'If'n you don't mind, I'll sorta roll out my bedroll in the timber by the barn. Then I'll light out in the mornin'.'

'You'll be coming in for breakfast first, won't you?'

'Well, yeah. Thanks. Yeah, I could do that. Then I gotta get back to trackin' that feller.'

Harvey looked at him for a long moment. Then, as matter-of-factly as talking of the weather, he said, 'He'll kill you. You know that. You know that don't you?'

A cold chill shivered its way the length of Jed's spine. He swallowed. 'I 'spect he might at that,' he agreed.

'But you'll track him anyway?'

Jed nodded. 'It's just somethin' I gotta do. I guess maybe dyin' wouldn't be as bad as not doin' it.'

That cold chill in his spine shivered again, as though it knew something of what lay ahead of him.

4

Jed fought to control his ragged breathing. His elbows dug into the carpet of dry pine needles. An unnoticed pine cone dug into his stomach as he crawled across it. He resisted the urge to turn over and toss it aside.

Crawling was more work than he anticipated. It was uphill. The altitude was higher than he was accustomed to and he needed to suck in great gulps of air, but he dared not; he had to breathe slow and steady. Be perfectly quiet. Take your time!

Slowly, inch by inch, he worked himself forward. He studied the ground in front of him, quietly picked up a dry branch and moved it from his path. He set it down softly in the pine needles, careful to make no noise.

He spent fifteen minutes crawling forward the next ten feet. At last he could push aside the pine seedling in front of him, and see his quarry.

He eased his .30/.30 carbine slowly out ahead of him. He took a full minute to move the gun silently into position. When it was just right, he squinted down the barrel at the scene below him.

Below and in front of him, just at the bottom of the slope, the burly, bearded outlaw squatted over a small fire. The smell of boiling coffee wafted on the breeze. It wakened a deep craving in Jed. Boy, he could use a cup of that! A skillet sat on the edge of the coals. Jed was so close he could hear the skillet sizzling softly.

He drew a bead on the centre of the outlaw's chest. He drew in a big breath. He barked, louder than he had intended to, 'Throw up your hands! You're under a — '

Whatever he had expected to happen, it was not what happened. At the first sound of his voice the outlaw hurled himself sideways. He rolled to his feet, his pistol already in his hand. He fired three times, faster than Jed could count, at the direction of the voice, then dived to the side.

Jed didn't even fire his rifle. Before he had even finished his call for surrender, the outlaw's fire had kicked dirt and pine needles into his face. He jerked back, pawing at his eyes.

He grabbed his rifle and rolled away, then crawled sideways into the trees. He stood up behind a large tree and rubbed at his eyes, trying to clear them of dirt and debris. Tears flooded them. His eyelids blinked rapidly of their own volition. Slowly they washed clear of foreign matter, and he was able to focus them again.

He peered carefully around his tree at the outlaw's camp. The coffee pot still sat on the fire. Steam billowed from it as it boiled. The skillet still sat on the coals, sizzling. Nothing else stirred.

Jed looked around wildly. Where had he gone? How could he move that fast? How could he shoot at the sound of a voice, and be that accurate? Where was he?

It dawned on him abruptly that he was now the hunted instead of the hunter. And that outlaw was far better equipped for the task than he! He eased back deeper into the timber, walking backwards, moving as soundlessly as possible. When he had moved fifty yards, he turned and began to walk forward, scanning the trees ahead for any sign of the bearded outlaw.

He hurried, forcing himself not to run. He moved in a large circle, trying to work his way back to where he had left his horse. He watched frantically in all directions, fighting to keep his breath slow and regular, lest the sound of puffing give away his position.

He moved to the bottom of the slope, over whose crown he had known the outlaw had pitched camp. He started up the opposite slope toward his horse. He moved more quickly, feeling a rising tide of panic welling up within him. He fought the urge to run headlong through the timber. Seeing a movement to his left out of the corner of his eye, he whirled and dropped to the ground with a thud. A grey squirrel scurried up the trunk of a tree and disappeared into the intertwining branches above.

He took a deep breath and stood slowly. He turned a complete circle, probing the timber with his eyes. He could see nothing out of place; he could hear no foreign sound, so he resumed his course toward his horse.

He peered carefully from around a large tree. His horse stood where he had left her, loosely tied to a thick stalk of a plum thicket. The animal gave no indication of anyone's presence, or any nervousness.

Jed stepped from behind the tree and walked swiftly to his mount. As he stepped from behind the tree, the horse's ears shot forward and she turned to watch her master's approach. I'm going to make it, Jed told himself silently.

He grabbed the reins and jerked

them free of the trunk of the plum bush, and swung into the saddle. He slid the rifle into the scabbard, then lifted the reins.

A shower of bark from the tree beside him sent slivers into the side of his face. On the heels of the unexpected pain a shot reverberated through the trees. He yelled and grabbed the side of his face.

The horse panicked and it was a good thing that it did. It leaped forward, dodging trees and brush. Jed grabbed the saddle horn, trying to keep his seat, making no effort to control the reins. Two more shots rang out. Once a small branch of a pine tree flew apart just at Jed's left.

Jed tried to gather his composure. He pulled himself forward, down on to the saddle horn, hugging his horse's neck. He still made no effort to control the animal. He was more than content to let her pick her own route and pace.

The horse was just as frightened as Jed. She was just as anxious to put distance between them and the source of her panic. It was one of those times horse and rider were truly of one mind.

The rollercoaster of Jed's emotions bottomed out. He fought to keep from sobbing as he hugged the horse's neck. Ten minutes ago, he had been so proud of himself; now the bottom had fallen out of everything.

The morning after his rescue of Nancy Walters he had breakfasted with the couple. Nancy insisted on getting out of bed to eat with them, and to thank Jed personally for saving her life. Her sharp features were less beautiful than Jed remembered, probably because of the pallor of her skin. Still, she was a strikingly beautiful woman, especially for a land where women were in as short supply as Wyoming. With less than one woman for every twelve men in the country, they were all beautiful.

She still had a severe headache, but was sure there would be no permanent damage. When Jed left there, he really felt like a hero for the first time in his life. He had been the dashing cowboy, saving the beautiful girl from certain death. Every boy's daydream had been fulfilled in that one glorious opportunity. Well, almost. This time, the girl already belonged to someone else. Nevertheless, he was a hero. It felt good. It felt great. It felt grand!

Then he had returned to his mission. He had found the outlaw's tracks from Nancy's description of the place she had been accosted. He recognized the trail of the horse he was riding at once. He would know those tracks wherever he saw them. He was not only a hero, he was a tracker! For the first time he actually began to believe he could track this man down and bring him to justice.

The tracks were not hard to follow. Even so, it was three days before Jed had gained enough ground to think about approaching the fugitive. It crossed his mind suddenly that the man didn't even know he was a fugitive. He didn't know Jed O'Dell was back there, hounding his trail, following with neither fear nor thought of giving up. Well, not too much fear.

He wasn't going to give up. He had accepted a mission. It was, finally, something that seemed right in his life. If he could do this one heroic deed, it would wipe away five years of being a failure. He could really be a hero. If he could be a hero, it wouldn't matter nearly so much that he had failed in the one most important thing fate had given him to do. He should have been this tenacious in working to avenge his family. He would have been, he told himself, if he had known who to pursue, who to track, who to bring to justice.

That was the difference: now he did know. He didn't know the man's name, but it didn't matter, he knew him; he knew what he was. He knew his personal habits by the trail those habits left behind. He knew his horse's track and he was gaining; he was closing in. He was about to be a hero again.

By sheerest luck he had ridden out

on a rimrock and surveyed the miles of country that lay below and before him. Just as he did, he spotted his quarry. The outlaw was nearly a mile away, and did not look up to see him watching as he began to pitch camp. It was an incredible stroke of luck. No, it couldn't be luck. It was fate! He had accepted the role of the Avenger of Blood. That shifted the weight of fate to his side. That had to be why he saw the campsite.

He studied the land around the outlaw's camp carefully and plotted a course that would bring him to the rim of the knoll overlooking the site. He could crawl up there, right on the rim of that knoll, and be less than thirty yards from the object of his quest. He would have the drop on him: the man would be helpless.

Then he could capture him, tie him to his saddle, and ride to the nearest town in triumph. He would be a hero. He would be the Avenger of Blood. But most important of all, he would atone for the failure to avenge his own family.

It had gone exactly as he had practised it in his mind. His approach had been right on target. His timing had been precise. He had crawled soundlessly to the exact vantage point he wanted and had called for the outlaw's surrender. What had gone wrong? How could a man react like that? As he fled in headlong panic from the one he had hunted so long, his euphoric mood gave way to a black despair.

It was the same as it had always been: he was a failure. He could not avenge anyone. He could not even capture a man he had a dead drop on, watching him in the sights of his rifle. He had started to speak. Then the man just disappeared from the rifle sight. It was as though he vanished into thin air. Then the man's own bullet had spewed dirt into his face. He couldn't have missed me more than two inches! Jed realized suddenly.

Slowly he collected his thoughts and

slowed his horse's headlong flight. He stopped and picked the slivers of pine bark from the side of his face. He mopped it gingerly with his neckerchief, looking at several small spots of blood. 'That was close!' he told his horse. 'Twice, he didn't miss me more'n inches. That man can shoot! An' he's quicker'n a bear swattin' trout out've a crick.'

He pushed his hat to the back of his head and scratched his right ear. 'Well, now what're we gonna do?' he asked his horse.

The horse tossed its head, jingling the bit ring. It offered no counsel. Jed turned the matter over in his mind. Finally he sighed heavily. 'Well, Rosie, let's find us a spot to camp. Come sun-up we'll get back on the trail. We found 'im onct, we'll find 'im agin. Only next time I'll be watchin' fer that there sorta thing. I'll get 'im somewheres where they ain't no place to run and dodge behind. Maybe I can even sneak up close enough to rap 'im over the head.'

He pondered the matter as they found a campsite of their own. After he had taken care of his horse, he made a small handful of fire. Over its flame he fixed himself some supper, then carefully put the fire out and crawled into his blankets.

One thing about it, he told himself. The Good Lord kept me from a-gettin' kilt today. That must mean I'm doin' the right thing, with this Avenger o' Blood thing. I'll keep after 'im.

But in his dreams he dodged bullets instead of avenging anything. Perhaps a man should listen to his dreams. They may be as much warning as worry.

5

Death-like silence gripped the saloon. Drinks were suspended between the bar and their owners' mouths. Cards were held frozen in mid-deal. Jed's soft words settled like a shroud, bringing all activity to a halt. 'I said, stand up. I'm takin' you to the sheriff.'

The burly outlaw, seated behind the table, stared in disbelief. He swore explosively. His full, black beard bristled. 'Who are you?'

'Don't matter none. I'm just the guy stopped you rapin' that there little ol' girl up along the Little Thunder.'

Confusion crossed the man's face. 'Little Thunder? Where's that?'

Jed gestured with his head. 'Up north fifty, sixty miles. Three weeks or a month ago.'

Recognition finally registered in the other's face. 'You! You're the dumb cowpoke that busted up my fun at that homestead! Now what in blazes are you doin'? 'Cept tryin' to get yourself kilt, that is.'

'I trailed you. A man like you can't be let free to run around. Not in a decent country. Now, get up, slow. I'm takin' you to the sheriff.'

'You ain't the one that pulled down on me in camp, up along Cow Crick, by any chance?'

'That was me. Now get up. I ain't gonna give you a chance to duck 'n run like you did then.'

The silence deepened, as though every occupant of the saloon held his breath. The outlaw eyed the carbine in Jed's hand. It was held at waist level. Its unflinching muzzle lined up with the centre of his. It seemed not to frighten him in the least. 'What's your name, kid?'

'Don't matter none,' Jed replied, then offered it anyway. 'Jed O'Dell. What's yours?'

The outlaw laughed unexpectedly.

'You don't even know who I am? You been houndin' my trail for 'most a month, an' you don't even know my name? My name's Bartholomew Shaw, boy,' he grinned. 'Bart, mostly. Ever hear the name?'

'Can't say as I have. Stand up. Nice and slow.'

Bart's eyes mirrored his disappointment, but he didn't move. 'You don't want me to do that,' he rasped. 'If I stand up, you'll die. You ain't nowheres near man enough to take Bart Shaw to the sheriff, boy. I've killed better men than you before breakfast. I can draw and shoot you, right between the eyes, before you can squeeze the trigger of that rifle. As a matter o' fact, I'll have three bullets in you before you even know I've reached for my gun. Now get out of here. Leave me alone, while you still can.'

Jed did not answer. Instead his thumb pulled back the hammer of the carbine. It cocked with an audible click. A rustle of movement betrayed men moving both directions away from the probable line of fire.

Bart glowered. 'Don't be stupid,' he rumbled. 'That girl ain't worth your time or mine. I didn't even get to use her none, thanks to you. It wouldn'ta hurt her none if I had. That's what they're for, and that's why I use 'em. But I ain't like some: I just use 'em, and then I ride on and leave 'em be, so the next man can have his fun too. Now put that gun away and get out of here.'

Jed's expression gave no indication he even heard. He said, 'You got till I count to three. If you ain't standin' when I hit three, I'll kill you where you sit.'

Muscles bunched at the hinge of Bart's jaw. 'You ain't gonna kill nobody. You ain't got it in you.'

'One.'

'Don't be a fool, boy. I'd soonest not have to kill you.'

'Two.'

'All right. All right. I'm standin'. Here's my hands. I'm standin' up now, nice 'n slow. Just don't go gettin' itchy on that trigger.'

Bart held his hands out in front of him, palms downward. He stood slowly, pushing the chair backward with the backs of his knees. He stepped sideways from in front of the chair, then took a step back from the table.

Jed was watching the man's eyes, instead of his hands. Somebody had told him that was the thing to do. Somebody was wrong. He never saw him start to draw. He never even saw any indication he was about to draw. His first flicker of awareness of danger was seeing Bart's gun clearing the leather of its holster. He squeezed the trigger of the .30/.30 as he flung himself sideways.

He felt a searing, burning sensation in his left shoulder as he felt the recoil of the rifle in his hands. The floor struck him hard on the right shoulder. He forced himself to a sitting position and levered another shell into the rifle. He was aware of the sound of shattering glass, but he was under the edge of a table. He could not see the man he had entered the saloon to arrest or kill.

He rolled to his right and came to his feet. The window behind the table where Bart had been sitting was shattered. Jed ran to it, to poke his head outside.

As soon as his head approached the broken window he realized it would be suicide. He tried to check his momentum, but it was too late. He knew his head would be exposed outside before he could stop.

Reacting quickly, he plunged forward instead, diving through the window head first. As he did, he heard the angry buzz of a bullet pass above his head. The roar of a pistol followed instantly. He landed again on that same shoulder. Pain coursed through him.

He lunged to his feet and levered another shell into the chamber. He braced himself for the impact of a bullet into his body. It did not come. There was nothing. He looked wildly about him. The opening between the saloon and the building next door was empty. The narrow section of street visible from where he stood was just as vacant.

Sudden hoofbeats from a horse spurred to a dead run carried from the street. He lowered the hammer on the rifle and ran to the front corner of the saloon. There was no sign of Shaw. The horse Jed had trailed all the way from Little Thunder Creek was gone. He cursed himself silently.

He ran down the street to the end of the row of stores and businesses. Dust hung in the air, but there was no sign of the fleeing outlaw. He stood there staring at nothing for a long moment. His emotions, once again, hit bottom.

Moving much more slowly, he retraced his steps until he was once again standing in front of the saloon. He felt strange. The normal noises of a town seemed to be absent. There was a strange roaring in his ears. He stopped, trying to think. What was wrong?

He realized suddenly that his left shoulder was on fire. He looked down. He was shocked to see the whole arm of his shirt soaked with blood. Realization washed across his mind, clearing away the confusion. 'He shot me!' he marvelled.

The occupants of the saloon had poured out on to the boardwalk. They stood in a tight knot watching him. Nobody spoke. Finally Jed spoke to nobody in particular. 'He shot me! I been shot. Is there a doctor in town?' he asked.

The man in the front of the group answered immediately. 'Doc Ringer's got an office right across the street. His buggy's there, so he ain't gone off nowheres.'

Jed followed the line of the man's point. He picked out the doctor's office at once. 'Much obliged,' he said.

He was getting light-headed by the time he made it across the street. The roaring was back in his ears. He couldn't seem to hear anything past it.

He opened the door and stumbled inside.

The doctor lost no time with idle words. He seated Jed in a chair, ripped the bloody shirt off, and began at once to clean the wound.

'You're lucky, my friend,' the doctor said, adjusting his glasses. 'The bullet ploughed a nice path through your shoulder, but appears not to have penetrated the chest cavity at all, or to have shattered any bones. I'm afraid it will be sore for a while, though. And you will be weak. You have lost a lot of blood, for such a short time. The bullet opened a lot of veins, and an artery. It seems not to have severed that artery, though. That's fortunate for you, you know.'

The doctor began to arrange instruments. He gave Jed some bitter tasting medicine. Suddenly, three shots rang out from down the street, followed by the sound of a horse, spurred to a dead run. Jed lunged from his chair and started for the door. The room abruptly spun around him. His face felt as though it were pressed against something. It was several seconds before he realized it was the floor. Then blackness overwhelmed him.

★ ★ ★

Sensation returned slowly. He seemed to be floating. He was surrounded by white softness he could only identify as clouds. He turned his head. His eyes met the most beautiful face he had ever seen. Deep-blue eyes twinkled at him above a bridge of freckles that crossed a small nose. A perfectly shaped face smiled from within a frame of light, reddish-brown curls. The curls cascaded onto shoulders garbed in a light blue gingham.

'Are . . . are you an angel?' Jed muttered.

The question was met by a delighted giggle. 'If you were dead, are you sure it would be an angel you'd see?' she asked.

Jed realized with a rush he was lying in a bed, with real linen sheets. He stammered, 'I-I'm sorry! I-I thought I must be dead. I thought this here was a cloud or somethin'. These is sheets, ain't they? I ain't never been in no real sheets like this here. They're so soft, like a cloud. But you're purty enough to be an angel. Who are you? Where am I?'

She giggled again. 'I'm Della. I'm Doctor Ringer's daughter. Now please lie quietly. You've been shot, you know.'

Memory returned with a rush. 'They was some other shots, after I was here. What happened?'

Her eyes clouded with concern. 'The man you tried to arrest in the saloon circled around and came back into town. He went down to the mercantile store. He got some supplies. Then he robbed Mr McPherson instead of paying for the things. Then he shot him and Henry both, that's Mr McPherson's clerk. He shot Mr McPherson twice. He died. Henry is alive, and he may recover. That's how we know what happened. Who was that man?'

Jed sighed. 'It's my fault. I just went an' messed it up agin. I always seem to do that. If I'd just shot him in the saloon, he wouldn'ta kilt them. But I just couldn't do that. It just didn't seem like the Christian thing to do, to just walk in there an' shoot 'im down. But I guess I shoulda. Now they ain't no tellin' what else he'll do afore I'm able to go after 'im.'

'Who is he? Why are you chasing him?'

Jed tried to sit up. Stabbing pain and a wave of dizziness quickly made him think better of it. He sighed and waited for the faintness to pass, then answered. 'His name's Bart Shaw. That's about all I know. He came on to a homestead up along Little Thunder Crick. He beat up a little fifteen-year-old girl there. Tried to rape 'er. I happened along an' stopped 'im, but he got away. I been trailin' 'im.'

'Why? Are you a lawman?

'No, I ain't no lawman.'

Her expression abruptly grew cold and grim. 'Are you a bounty hunter?'

'No! I don't even know if there's any bounty on him. I just chanced on to the thing. Somebody's gotta stop him. If he did that to her, he's done it to others. He'll keep on till someone stops him.'

Her face mirrored her confusion. 'Why should it be you? Do you know the girl?'

He shook his head. 'Her name's Allie, that's all I know. I don't even know what her last name is. I 'spect she's got one, though. I just happened along.'

'You don't even know her last name? Then why should it be you?' she asked again.

He groped for words to explain, and quickly despaired of being able to. 'Hard to explain,' he mumbled. 'Somebody's gotta do it. I got nothin' better to do.'

Her eyes flashed fire. 'Stop it! I will not tolerate being treated like that! I may just be the spoiled daughter of the finest frontier doctor in Wyoming, but I am not a complete idiot! People do not risk their lives trailing and trying to arrest some desperate outlaw just because they have nothing better to do. If you don't wish to tell me your business, that is your privilege, but do not treat me like a child or an idiot.'

He flushed. 'I didn't mean to sound like that, ma'am. It's just too hard to explain. I ain't that good with words.'

She sighed. 'Typical cowboy. You can talk to your horse, but you can't talk to me.'

'I'd a whole lot rather talk to you,' he protested at once. 'It's just that you'd think I'm crazy or somethin'.'

'Try me.'

He was silent a long time. Maybe it was the pain; maybe it was whatever the doctor had given him to relieve the pain. He still felt like he was floating. His tongue suddenly felt looser than he could ever remember. He wanted to talk: he needed to talk. He suddenly felt as if all the unspoken words in his life were piled up behind his teeth, pressing those restraints like too much water behind a fragile dam. Then the dam burst. A gushing avalanche of words seemed to tumble over each other in their haste to get out.

'It was more'n five years ago. I was all growed up and gone from home. I come home one time after we was all done weanin' calves on the Double Bar Six. That's the spread I was workin' on. I'm a top-notch cowpoke. Anyways, when we was done weanin', I took off for home. I hadn't been home fer 'most a year.

'My folks had a small place along Clear Crick. I seen a whole flock o' magpies and buzzards, well afore I got there. When I rode into the yard I found my whole family dead. Ma and Bertie was a'lyin' out in the middle o' the yard. They didn't have a stitch o' clothes on. They'd been raped somethin' awful. They was all over blood, on their legs and such. Bertie especially. She was just fifteen, too. They'd been shot, then. Right between the eyes.

Both of 'em. The gun what shot 'em was so close it burned all the hide off'n their foreheads, like he stuck the gun right up to their heads and pulled the trigger.

'Pa was lyin' right in the door o' the barn. He'd been shot six or eight times. It looked like he'd heard somethin' and come a'runnin' to the door of the barn, and they just shot him to pieces. He didn't even have a gun on 'im.'

'Oh, my land sakes! Oh, my word! Oh, how awful! Who did it?' Della breathed.

The doctor must have given him something to dull the pain, he decided. It was the first time he could remember trying to talk about it, that he could actually say what he felt. He shook his head. 'Never could find out. I tried. Lord knows I tried. I tried to track 'em, but I lost 'em on the main road. I tried to learn to be a gunman, but I ain't no good at it. Just ain't got it in me. I tried to be some kind of detective or somethin', and I asked questions for a year, but I couldn't never get no line on who done it at all. I wanted to find 'em so bad I couldn't sleep for thinkin' about it. I had this awful ache inside of me here, and it didn't never go away. I knowed I'd have to find who did it, that I couldn't really face myself till I did, but I couldn't even find out who to look for. If'n I had, they'd've just kilt me, I 'spect. I ain't no good with a gun.'

'You mean this man isn't even one of the ones who did that? Then why are you chasing this man?'

'I was made the Avenger of Blood.'

'The what?'

'Like in the Bible. The Avenger of Blood.'

'I know that's in the Bible, but I always thought that was a close relative of the person that was killed or, or . . . whatever.'

'I was just appointed to be the Avenger of Blood for that girl.'

'Who appointed you?'

'Her mother.'

'How could she do that?'

'I don't know. She just did it. She just said it. She said, 'I appoint you the Avenger of Blood, to track down and arrest or kill that man'.'

'And you accepted that?'

'It sounded like some holy sorta thing, the way she said it. Seemed the only thing to do.'

'Why?'

He was silent for a long while. When he spoke he felt as though he suddenly understood himself better than he ever had. 'I ain't sure I understand that, but maybe I'm sorta beginnin' to. I been real 'shamed ever since I found 'em all, like that. Ma and Pa and Bertie, I mean. 'Shamed that I hadn't done nothin' about it. Oh, I buried 'em an' all, an' prayed over 'em as best I could, but I didn't never find out who did it, and didn't never do nothin' about it. Oh, I tried. I just couldn't. I ain't never got that picture outa my head. Ever' time I close my eyes, seems like, I see 'em there. All a'lyin' in the yard.

'Then I come along Little Thunder

82

Crick, an' the same sorta thing was just startin' to happen. It was like when I rode onto this thing, I was all at once given a chance to make up for what I couldn't do for my own family. I did know who it was what done this — I knowed what he looked like; I knowed what way he went. I could follow this guy. I could keep him from doin' it to others. I could do what needed done. I figgered if I did, I could finally hold my head up and not be 'shamed no more. Or else maybe he'd kill me for tryin', and then I wouldn't feel 'shamed no more anyway. Either one would be better than just havin' the shame. Anyways, I did keep 'im from a'doin' it to one other girl. Well, I guess I didn't rightly keep 'im from it. She done got away, but he was chasin' her, I reckon. Then she went an' got throwed by her horse, and hung up in her stirrup, and her horse was a'draggin' 'er to death. I done caught 'er horse an' got 'er loose. I tooked 'er home. She had a husband.'

'You saved her life?'

He didn't know why the question didn't embarrass him. It must be the medicine he was given. 'Yes, ma'am. Sorta like one o' them hero fellas, you know. It felt plumb good inside, an' they was plumb awful grateful, an' they called me a hero. I din't feel like no hero, but they kept on a'sayin' I was one anyway. Anyhow, then I lit out on his trail agin. Till it come here. Now he done got away from me agin.'

She stared at him for several moments. 'Then you will chase him again, if the posse doesn't catch him?'

He nodded. He felt as though he were speaking some sacred oracle as he answered. 'I'll follow him to the ends of the earth, if I have to. I'll find him. I'll bring 'im back, either tied up or laid acrost 'is saddle. Or else he'll kill me.'

'Or he will kill you,' she echoed.

Something in her voice sounded more prophetic than simply worried. He shrugged his shoulders. 'What may be as may be,' he said.

As soon as the words were out of his

mouth he noticed how much like his mother they sounded. He bit his lip and turned his face away from Della.

He didn't really hear Della's response. He was suddenly so tired! Her voice was soothing, but it was beginning to fade into the distance, it seemed. It merged into some vision of a home and family, and the dream gave way to deep sleep.

Della sighed heavily, rose from her chair and walked quietly from the room.

6

The bullet was totally unexpected.

An experienced lawman is always alert to unexpected threats. Jed was neither experienced nor a lawman. He was too exhilarated to feel any sense of danger. This was where he felt he was at his best. He was a tracker! The trail that was too faint and cold for nearly anyone else to follow, was as clear as words on a printed page were to book readers. It had been a long chase. Too long.

He had asked what seemed an endless number of people the futile questions, until finally he had struck pay dirt. Many people think that in a sparsely settled country, a man can easily get lost. Quite the opposite is true. In a country where few people live, everyone knows everyone else. When a stranger rides through, it is a thing to note; it is a thing to remember.

When Jed encountered someone who had seen Bart Shaw ride through, that person remembered. He remembered what way he went. He remembered what horse he was riding. That led to the next person who remembered, then the next. Finally the trail was fresh enough to find the tracks he remembered so well: the tracks of Shaw's horse he could follow anywhere. It had taken a long time. It had covered a lot of miles. Now he was closing in.

Then a bullet changed everything. The horse beneath him shuddered suddenly. The sound of a rifle shot slapped against his ears. His head jerked up, even as he felt the horse stumble. He was vaguely aware of a wisp of smoke from the edge of the trees 250 yards away, then his horse collapsed beneath him. He jerked his feet from the stirrups and tried to roll clear, grabbing for the rifle in the saddle scabbard.

He managed to roll free as the horse went down, but the rifle was pinned between the animal and the ground. Jed's grip on the stock flipped him over. His head crashed against a rock. Blackness engulfed him.

He had waited nearly a month after being shot before setting out on the trail of the wanton outlaw. He didn't really need a month for his shoulder to heal. Within the first week he felt as fit as ever, except for being weak from loss of blood. The arm bothered him very little, except for being stiff and sore. No sign of infection invaded the wound.

Della was the reason he was so reluctant to leave. He had never felt the things that surged within him whenever she was near. For the first time he could remember, he became conscious of his appearance. Tattered sleeves and trousers suddenly embarrassed him. The ring of greasy dirt around the band of his hat looked suddenly ugly and filthy. He had spent almost half of his reserve of cash money on clothes to impress her. It seemed to work. He could see the delight that began to grow in her eyes whenever he walked in.

He had started with a haircut and shave and bath. Then he had purchased a couple of pairs of the new style pants, made of some material that seemed almost like light canvas. Levi something, the clerk called them. He assured him they were the latest thing. They did fit well. Better than any pants he'd ever owned. He bought two silk shirts, with neckerchiefs made of the same material. Then he added a new vest of suede leather, and a new hat. It was hard to believe how much money it added up to when he picked out the hat. It was worth every penny.

'Why, Jed O'Dell, you're as dandied up as a dude at a barn dance,' she had teased him.

'Can't impress an angel lookin' like the devil,' he had countered.

Then he thought of how very clever that sounded. His chest swelled with pride. He had never said anything that sounded that good in his life.

He even considered looking for a job

close by, so he could just stay there. After all, what right did Allie's mother have to name him, a perfect stranger, a . . . what was it? He had almost forgotten the term, thinking about Della all the time. Avenger of Blood, that's what she called it.

Even as he argued with himself, he knew he had to keep to his quest. He couldn't pretend it had faded that far from his consciousness. He wasn't sure he wanted to. Trailing Bart had given him the first real relief he had felt from his sense of failure in more than five years. He had not realized how deeply not avenging his family affected him, until he had encountered this chance to atone for it vicariously. Now he had even more reason to succeed. He had to give Della a reason to be proud of him! It was no longer enough just to be a hero: he had to be her hero!

'I don't understand why you think it's your responsibility,' she had told him, 'but I have to admit, I really admire your strength of character. I know you'll carry through with it. You'll come back here, then, won't you?'

After that, nothing would be able to prevent it! If he lived, he'd be back.

When the murder of the mercantile store owner occurred, the town marshal had quickly organized a posse. They left town in a huge cloud of dust, but raising a few hopes and a lot of dust was all they accomplished. The posse had returned to town the third day. They had followed and trailed Shaw to the Platte River, but had lost the trail there. They had followed both banks of the river for several miles, but weren't able to find his tracks leaving the water.

Jed listened carefully to everything they had to say. From the direction of the man's flight, and from the supplies he took before shooting McPherson, he had a hunch where Shaw was heading. He was sure he was capable of finding and following his trail, even after it was cold. After all, he was a better tracker than anyone he knew before this all started. Besides, he had been learning fast.

Once he found the people who pointed him the right way, he was like a bloodhound. The trail was there. There was little chance rain would wash it away. Early September in Wyoming is not notable for rainy weather. The next moisture would most likely be in the form of snow, and there was no indication any break in the hot weather would provide that anytime soon.

Still, he shouldn't have waited so long. The trail was harder to pick up than he had supposed. He had assumed everyone who saw Shaw would remember. He hadn't counted on the outlaw staying away from any settlement or homestead for so long. But nobody could disappear forever.

Once he found the trail, he gained ground quickly. The outlaw would spend one or two days in a particularly good place watching for pursuit. Then he would move on, and when he found another good lookout spot, he would stay for a day or two again. He acted as if he knew pursuit would come. He just didn't know when, and he was determined to keep a trap set for whenever it did. Realization of what the outlaw was doing sent a cold shiver up Jed's back. He suddenly felt as if a dozen pairs of eyes were watching every move he made. He began to jump every time a sage hen took off abruptly, or a crow cawed unexpectedly.

For three weeks he kept gaining rapidly. They entered the mountains following Elkhorn Creek. Then he saw sign of a remarkably different tone. Shaw's horse had slipped on a loose stone and slid one hoof into a narrow crevice between two rocks. The momentum of the slip and the weight of the big outlaw had created a sideways force greater than the strength of the leg bone. It snapped half way between hock and knee.

Jed sat in his saddle and studied the dead animal. It had been eaten on by magpies and buzzards, and probably at least one coyote, by the look of things. From the work they had done on the carcass, he estimated he had found the horse two or three days after it happened. He studied the sign in the surrounding area carefully. He saw the indications the outlaw had stripped saddle, bridle and pack from the animal, and transferred it on to another horse.

'Now where'd he get another horse?' Jed asked.

He decided to backtrack the new animal to answer that question first. He didn't have to trail it far. Less than two miles up the creek he came to the camp of a trapper. He had been shot in the back, his heart shattered by the bullet that tore through him. He never saw it coming. 'Probably didn't even feel it,' Jed mused.

The camp was ransacked. The hapless trapper never knew he had provided the fleeing outlaw with both provisions and a new horse.

Jed took time to bury the man's

remains before pressing on. Now he was less than two days behind, and closing quickly. He should have been more careful; he should have known an outlaw as experienced as Shaw would still be watching his back-trail. He had marvelled at how often Shaw set a trap for pursuit, waiting for days sometimes, watching his own tracks. Jed should have watched much more carefully. He should have trailed from as far to one side as he could see the sign. He should have done a dozen things differently. He didn't.

When the shot came that felled his horse and knocked him unconscious, it came as a complete surprise.

He slowly became aware of a pounding pain in his head. Then he heard the buzzing of the flies. He couldn't have been unconscious more than half an hour, but already they were drawn to the blood from his horse's wound, and from his own head.

He groaned and rolled over, coming to his hands and knees. He let his head hang until the dizziness passed. Then he looked around.

There was no sign of Shaw. There was no indication he had made any effort to finish Jed off. That fact fought to work its way through the haze that hindered his mind. Then the reason struck him, pounding at him past the pain of his head.

'He saw me get conked and knows I'm hurt. He's just left me hurt and afoot in the mountains,' he said. 'He just left me to die slow.'

He staggered to the creek and plunged his head into the icy water. The shock cleared some of the fog from his brain. He washed the blood from his hair, and felt the gash on the back of his head gingerly. 'Not too bad, don't feel like. I've been busted worse.'

He got to his feet slowly. Waiting until the wave of dizziness passed, he walked back to his dead horse. He unfastened the cinch, then sat down on the ground. Bracing his feet against the back of the dead animal, he pulled the right stirrup and the cinch from under her, freeing the saddle. Then he lay back on the ground to wait for the dizziness to pass again. It passed. Then, more slowly, the pounding, throbbing pain in his head subsided to a bearable level.

When it did, he removed the bridle as well. From the saddle-bags he removed his supply of jerky, hardtack, matches, ammunition for both pistol and rifle, and a few other things. He wrapped them in his slicker, making a sack of it that would carry easily.

Taking a length of rope from his saddle-bag, he tied one end around a fist-sized stone. He gripped the rope about three feet from the stone, and began to whirl it around. He threw it up and over a tree branch, hanging on to it so the weight of the stone wouldn't pull it clear over.

He hung the bridle on the saddle horn, looping the reins in a coil around the pommel. Then he tied the end of the rope to the saddle horn. He threw the stirrups and cinch straps over the saddle, to make as small a package of it as possible. Then he hoisted the saddle up, leaving it hanging from the tree branch, nearly ten feet from the ground. He tied the other end of the rope to the tree trunk, as high as he could reach.

'That oughta keep the porkypines from chewin' it to pieces afore I come back for it,' he said with satisfaction.

'Now I gotta think,' he said. 'My head hurts too much. Gotta think anyway. If I foller the crick all the way down to the Platte, I can probably walk out in two or three weeks, even in these boots. Trouble is, Shaw might camp thataway, just to see if I do. Or he might set some sort o' traps fer me. Matter o' fact, he must think there's some reason I couldn't walk out thataway, or he'da finished me off while I was out.'

He turned a slow circle, studying the lay of the land. Then he continued his soliloquy. 'If I leave the crick and climb up over that ridge south and east, I won't have no guarantee o' water. They oughta be another crick in the next canyon over, though. If I remember right, it might be Shoe Crick. Then I could foller it. He wouldn't likely be 'spectin' me to do that.'

He nodded his head with decision. He looped his coiled lariat over his head and one shoulder. Carrying his rifle in his right hand, and the makeshift bag of provisions in his left, he set out at right angles to the creek.

It took him the rest of the day to climb to the top of the ridge. At the top he fell to the ground, panting and exhausted. 'Dang boots ain't made for walkin', that's fer sure,' he puffed.

The sun had disappeared. The temperature at this elevation dropped dramatically as soon as it did. He could already feel the chill creeping into him.

'Didn't even think to bring no blankets or bedroll,' he lamented. 'What a greenhorn stunt! And I don't 'spect I'd oughta start no fire. Ain't no tellin' where Shaw is.'

He spotted a small patch of lush vegetation with a different coloration than the surrounding fauna. 'You don't s'pose that there's a spring?' he queried.

Walking quickly, he found a tiny trickle of water seeping out from under a large rock. Following it down the side of the slope, he found a place where rocks formed a small pool, several inches deep and nearly a foot across.

'Well bless my soul,' he exulted. 'I don't hafta make a dry camp.'

He drank deeply of the ice-cold liquid. Then he removed the contents of the bag/slicker. He ate a couple of cold hard biscuits and a healthy piece of jerky. Then he put the slicker on, and curled up beneath the cover of a juniper. He was asleep almost at once.

He was awake and up with the first probing rays of light. Moving about warmed him enough to stop him shivering. He ate a repetition of his supper, made a sack of his slicker to hold his provisions again, and set out.

It was mid-afternoon when he came

out of the timber and saw a broad, grassy valley. A stream flowed placidly for a mile and a half, before resuming its tumbling course over the rocky mountainside. Along the banks of the stream blackberry and raspberry bushes sagged with ripe berries. Wasting no time, he hurried to the nearest bush and began eating hungrily.

From time to time he interspersed the berries with more of his jerky and dry biscuits. Then he forced himself to quit. 'If I ain't careful, I'm gonna physic myself somethin' awful.'

Then his eye caught sight of tracks on the far side of the stream. He laid his rifle and lariat carefully on the pile of his provisions, and waded the creek. 'Horses! Wild horses! There's a whole herd o' wild horses usin' this valley, and drinkin' outa this crick!'

He sat down and stared around him. His mind raced wildly. 'It's gonna take me two or three weeks, at least, to walk outa here,' he said, once again speaking aloud. 'If I can do it, in these boots, then I ain't gonna be able to walk for a month, while my feet heal up. But if I could catch me one o' them horses, maybe I could bust him enough to ride 'im outa here.'

The possibilities tumbled over each other in his mind. He thought of having to retrace his steps to retrieve his saddle, then carry it over the way he had come. That would be no easy task.

'At least I'd have my bedroll then. I'd best go get it afore I try to catch a horse, though,' he said, 'otherwise I'd have to try to keep 'im tied up for two days while I'm gone, and he'd most likely get loose, or hurt hisself fightin' the rope.'

It took him three days, instead of the two he had counted on. One day was sufficient to retrace his steps and get his gear. It took twice as long, however, for him to return. Part of it was the added weight; part of it was the toll on his feet and legs from walking in boots that were only made for riding.

With the rest of his provisions

collected, he set up a little more elaborate base camp. He shot a deer, dropping him with his first shot. 'Whatd'ya know about that!' he said. 'First time I ever got one with the first shot! Maybe I am gettin' help from somewheres. Maybe bein' an Avenger o' Blood gives a feller some sort o' pertection.'

He gorged himself on fresh venison, hanging both haunches high up from a tree, out of reach of hungry animals. The weather might be cool enough at this elevation to keep the meat from spoiling for quite a while. Especially since it was hung in the shade.

Part of the meat he cut into thin strips. He hung them over a thin pole, arranged above a long, narrow fire that he kept tended. The meat cooked and smoked, effectively preserving it.

He was in no hurry now. He had to ensure his own survival, ahead of everything else. When he had a sufficient supply of food, he could begin to work on his main quest.

Anyway, his feet were far too sore to do anything right now.

After giving his feet a few days' rest to allow them to regain a semblance of normalcy, he began to stalk the herd of wild horses. Maybe, just maybe, they would hold the key to his survival.

On the other hand, a small voice in the back of his mind argued, he just might get himself killed trying to catch one.

7

He scarcely dared breathe. One sound, one movement, and his chances would melt like a snowflake in a teakettle. He might survive if he failed, but he couldn't be sure. The odds against it were too strong. Especially since he had already wasted so much time and energy. That made it a life or death effort this day.

Jed squatted in the edge of a plum bush. A thorny branch gouged into his back, but he dared not move to relieve the discomfort. He had several freshly cut branches from another plum bush tied to his legs, screening him from view. He could see through the leaves, but not easily. If he allowed enough opening to see clearly, he knew he could be seen as well.

He had scouted the herd of wild horses for a week. There were nearly thirty mares, about half of them with colts. They were ruled over and guarded by the finest wild stallion Jed had ever seen.

The stallion was, he guessed, ten or twelve years old. He was a deep sorrel, with a white blaze on his forehead and four perfectly matched stocking feet. Jed guessed the beautiful animal would stand sixteen hands high. He moved with a grace and power that made Jed ache to watch him.

Something in him yearned to put a rope on that stallion, to master him, to claim him, to prove his ability to capture and tame the best and the strongest. On that horse, he would be the envy of every cowboy in Wyoming, but he was far too practical to make the attempt. He was very well aware how difficult it would be to ever break a wild stallion that age. To try to do so in the open, with no one to help, with no other horse to fall back on, would be utter foolishness. Nevertheless, Jed watched him, drooled, and dreamed.

He had figured out something of the herd's routine, and guessed where and when they would come to the stream for water. If he was right, some of them would pass by mere feet from where he squatted in hiding today. It was the right day. The wind was perfect to keep his scent carried away from them. If he made no noise, no movement to betray his presence, one of the mares just might pass close enough for him to rope.

He had already been in place, waiting, for more than two hours. His legs hurt. His back ached. His neck and face itched fiercely. Sweat tickled as it ran down his stomach and ribs. Still, he dared not move. He scarcely dared breathe.

Then he saw the head of the magnificent stallion appear over the crest of the hill, 300 yards away. The animal stopped, silhouetted at the top of the hill and surveyed the area, the breeze ruffling his mane and tail. He tossed his head and stamped the ground once, then he lowered his head and began cropping grass.

Within minutes several of the mares came into view. They were spread out, grazing their way toward the creek. Two colts frolicked, chasing each other in circles.

More and more of the horses came into view. The stallion trotted to the bank of the creek and buried his muzzle in the clear cold stream. He lifted his head and looked around, ever vigilant. The sun flashed from the droplets of water that scattered from his chin, as though diamonds were being strewn by this king of his realm. He lowered his head again, cropping the lush grass from the creek bank.

One of the mares broke off eating and began walking toward the creek. Her path was perfect to bring her within feet of where Jed squatted in wait. She appeared to be four or five years old. She was sorrel and white pinto, with a broad chest and full neck. Her legs were slightly thicker than most, but not blocky.

Another mare fell into line behind her, following her to the water. The second mare was a dun, smaller, with fine legs and a small head. First one'll sure be a handful, but she's a fine horse, Jed told himself silently. Let's go fer the good 'un.

The horses were intent on the water and the slaking of their thirst, their vigilance momentarily allowed to flag. Otherwise, they never would have gotten that close without noticing something out of place in the oddly shaped plum bush.

When they were less than fifteen feet from him, Jed stepped forward and whirled his rope once, and cast it without hesitation. The startled horse whirled her head at his first movement. She set her feet and spun away from him. Before she could make her first lunge, the loop settled over her head.

Jed wrapped the end of the rope around his right hand. He turned sideways to the horse, bracing his feet widely apart. He braced his hand against his hip, to use his whole body to resist the force of the frightened animal. With his left hand he gripped the rope.

The mare uttered a shriek of fear and anger. The whole herd of horses thundered away in a cloud of dust. Jed clung desperately to the rope. The strength of the wild animal was tremendous. She lunged across the gentle slope, bucking and plunging against the strange restraint that had settled around her neck. She dragged Jed, his feet digging twin furrows in the ground, powerless to stop her. The plum branches he had tied to his legs were ripped painfully away.

The mare realized suddenly she was abandoned by the rest of the herd. She turned to follow them. The turn brought her in a half circle, nearer to Jed. It put slack in the rope that provided him the opportunity he needed.

He lunged toward a small pine tree, with a trunk about six inches in diameter. He took a quick dally around the trunk, gripped the end of the rope, and leaned into it.

The mare hit the end of the slack. The rope tightened, but the dally offered no compromise. Her neck stopped abruptly at the end of the rope. The rest of her body catapulted over her head and crashed to the ground with a resounding thud. Dust boiled up from the impact.

Jed quickly took a second dally around the tree and waited for the wild mare to regain her feet. She did at once, and plunged off again toward the fleeing herd. She hit the end of the rope and was spilled again, just as hard as before.

She struggled to her feet again. This time she plunged off at right angles to the way she had ran before. The results, however, were the same. She was slammed into the ground once more, as unceremoniously and painfully as the first two times.

This time she regained her feet more

slowly. She backed against the tether of the rope, and strained against it. Her ears were laid back flat against her head. Her nostrils flared. Her eyes rolled wildly. She braced her feet and pried against the pull of the rope with all her strength.

The rope creaked and groaned, but it held. The mare's eyes began to bulge. Pulling against the rope also shut off her supply of air. Jed watched her carefully. The mare refused to relent in her attempts to pull away. Her eyes began to glaze over.

As she began to totter, Jed released the pressure on the rope. The mare fell sideways. She lay where she had fallen, gasping in great gulps of air.

While she was there, Jed replaced the dallies of his rope around the tree. After nearly three minutes, the mare struggled to her feet again. She stood spraddle-legged, glaring at Jed. Her nostrils were again flared and her ears laid back in angry defiance. She started backing again, until she was once again leaning against the unrelenting pull of the rope.

This time, however, when it began to choke, she tossed her head and took a step forward. Jed immediately took up the slack. He backed away from the tree, holding the end of the rope, keeping it arranged on the tree so she would not be able to jerk it from his hands.

The mare suddenly started to trot forward, in a line that would bring her within fifteen feet of the tree. Jed backpedalled quickly, to keep the slack out of the rope. By the time the mare passed the tree, he had taken up almost half the rope.

The rope tightened against the mare's neck. She squealed again, and angrily lunged against it. There was more moderation in her anger already, though. She did not throw herself at the end of the rope, it only spun her around, and she stood, spraddle-legged, again leaning against its pull.

She realized at once that she was

choking herself, and lessened the pull just enough to allow herself to breathe. She stood there, braced against it as hard as she could and still breathe, glaring at this sudden enemy who had her in his control.

Jed approached the mare with infinite patience. He was talking now, still holding tightly to the end of the rope. She squealed and sidled away from him. He kept approaching, crooning softly to her. Every time she moved closer to the tree, he pulled the slack from the rope.

Within two hours the horse had worked up to the point within three feet of the tree, where she was secured. Two wraps of the rope around the tree had allowed Jed to keep pulling the slack up, while not allowing her to take any of it back.

Jed didn't stop crooning to the frightened animal. He worked his way in slowly, as the mare backed around and around the tree, to within touching distance of her. The first time he touched her, she flinched away violently and squealed her fright. Little by little he worked beyond her fear. Soon she began to snort and jerk away, instead of squealing in panic. Then even that began to abate, until she allowed his hand to remain on her shoulder.

The skin jerked and twitched and quivered under his touch. He kept crooning softly. He stroked the sweating, jerking hide gently. 'Eeeasy girl,' he kept saying, in that soft monotone. 'Eeeasy there. Eeeasy girl. I'm not gonna hurt you. You're a fine horse. A fine horse. Eeeasy now. See, I'm not hurting you a bit. Eeeasy.'

Carefully, slowly, he eased the loose end of the lariat around her neck. Then, careful to avoid any sudden moves, he tied it in a bowline knot, so it could not slip tight and choke her any more. Then he slipped his loop carefully over her head. To his surprise, she did not bolt and try to run as the loop passed over her head.

'You're gentlin' down awful quick, ol'

girl,' he crooned. 'I wonder if you're somebody's horse that got away from 'em some time or other. Are you, girl? Was you somebody's horse onct, afore you went wild? They didn't never brand you, if you was. You musta been purty young, but you sure act like you've been around people afore. I betcha have, ain't you? You ever been ridden, girl? You ever had a saddle on? I bet we's a'gonna find out.'

Finally, he sighed. It had been six hours since Jed had dabbed his rope on the startled and unsuspecting mare. He trembled with fatigue. 'You gotta be just as tired as I am, ol' girl,' he continued to croon. 'You gotta be plumb thirsty, too. You was goin' to water when I roped you. You figure you're wore out enough I can handle you, to take you to water?'

He unwrapped the rope carefully from the tree. He coiled the excess, then wrapped it once around his right hand to allow himself extra grip. Then he walked away from the tree and tugged on the rope.

At first the horse tossed her head and jerked back against the rope. Then she took a tentative step forward. She tugged against the rope, then took another step, then another. Then she decided she was loose, and began to trot away from Jed.

Jed braced his feet and wedged his hand against his hip, with the rope across the front of his hips. The rope tightened against the mare's neck. She wheeled and faced Jed. Her ears went back flat against her head again. Her nostrils flared. She glared defiantly at him. Then she tossed her head and took a step forward, slackening the rope.

'Well whatd'ya know,' Jed marvelled. 'You really was somebody's horse once. I just know you was. You're rememberin' too quick not to've been.'

It took another thirty minutes for Jed to get her to the creek, then another ten for her to begin to drink. When she finally did, she drank thirstily.

Dusk was thickening quickly. Jed worked the mare close enough to another tree that offered good grass all the way around it, and tied the rope securely to the trunk. Then he slaked his own thirst. He made himself some supper and forced himself to eat in spite of his fatigue. Then he moved his bedroll just out of reach of the mare's range of motion. He spread his blankets upwind, where she could smell his presence throughout the night. He was asleep before the blanket settled over him.

He woke once in the night to the insistent neighing of the stallion. The mare answered, and the stud approached to retrieve the lost member of his harem. Jed stood up and yelled. The mighty stud squealed, snorted and thundered away.

'She's mine now, big stud,' Jed called into the night.

He smiled as he drifted back into the pleasant world of sleep.

An hour later the stud was back,

dismayed at the loss of one of his brood. Jed stood and spoke again, once more sending the king of the range in sudden retreat. The mare neighed after him mournfully.

8

The horse shuddered. Jed crooned softly, constantly, saying nothing, but letting the animal hear his voice all the time. He stepped carefully into the saddle. He settled in deeply. He turned his toes outward, hooking his spurs in the cinch straps to help him hold his seat. He pulled his knees tightly beneath the swells of the pommel.

He leaned forward and jerked the shirt loose that he had tied around the mare's head for a blindfold. She shuddered again. Then he jerked the light rope loose that held her right hind foot tied up, preventing her ability to buck.

The skin along her back and sides twitched. She took a hesitant step forward. Then a second. Then she realized the restraints were gone. She squealed in anger and frustration. She ducked her head, humped her back, and leaped high in the air. At the crest of the leap, she twisted her back and kicked out with both hind feet. She came down with a bone-jarring jolt, twisted to the left and bucked again.

Jed held the reins with his left hand and gripped the saddle horn tightly with his right. He leaned back as far as his grip on the saddle horn would allow, staying balanced and in time with the horse's bucking, but keeping himself pulled deep in the saddle.

He was almost disappointed. He had expected a head-snapping, bone-jarring, arm-wrenching ride that would exact every ounce of strength and skill he had acquired on a hundred broncs or more. If he lost his seat, he was conscious of the need to keep his grip on the reins, so he wouldn't lose the horse, and his saddle and bridle as well. He was ready for the ride of his life, with the highest stakes for which he had ever ridden. It was, after all, his life that was on the line.

Instead, the mare bucked hard for six or eight jumps, then quit. She tossed her head and snorted a couple of times. She crow-hopped twice. Then she began to trot toward the distant tree-line. He was instantly impressed and surprised. She had as smooth and ground-eating a trot as Jed could remember riding.

'You sure was somebody's horse onct!' Jed exulted. 'You remember! You're rememberin' everything you knowed.'

He pulled the reins to one side and she responded instantly. He nudged her with his spurs, and she bounded forward, running full speed within four jumps. He turned her sharply, first right, then left. He put her through a series of manoeuvres that would have left a lesser horseman sitting in the grass. When he would spin her quickly, she would turn such a tight corner his inside foot would drag the ground. He pulled her to a stop, and she obeyed at once, squatting low in the rear and bracing her front legs stiffly in order to stop quick. She tossed her head, telegraphing her desire to perform some more.

'Wow!' Jed shouted. 'Did I ever catch myself a horse! Whoever you got away from lost the finest horse he ever owned, bar none. An' it warnt more'n two or three years ago, or you'da forgot more'n that.'

He still could not believe his good fortune. In the first three days after he caught the horse, she gentled to his touch. He was amazed at the speed of the process. Except during the times the persistent stallion returned to try to reclaim the mare he had lost from his herd, she had shown no strong desire to get away from him. By the third day she actually seemed to enjoy having him pet her, brush the burrs and stickers from her hair, groom and trim her mane and tail, and tend the several small abrasions on her legs. The fourth day she even allowed him to trim her hooves, something no truly wild horse would have done for weeks.

That was when he decided to rush breaking her to the saddle. If she had been that accustomed to human touch before escaping to run wild, it was possible she had even been ridden. Today's ride had verified it: he had a horse.

He stayed in the saddle for several hours. He rode to the top of a tall knoll he had spotted several days previously. He knew he would have a great view of the whole valley from there.

He was not disappointed. The panorama that spread out before him was so breathtakingly beautiful it brought tears to his eyes. Mountains rose to his left. Row after row of peaks, each row a little taller than the one in front, ranged to the west and south. Taller ones were white-capped with snow. The tops of all of them glistened as the sun bounced from granite faces and escarpments.

At the base of the nearest range of peaks, the creek he was camped beside meandered a crooked course the length of the lush valley. Bushes, still hanging thick with berries, lined both banks. Great cottonwood trees spread their immense boughs outward, shading areas of darker green. Back away from the creek, clumps of aspen sprouted from the ground. Their silver-backed leaves shivered and quaked at the slightest breeze, making the clumps of trees look like animated beings, each chattering to its nearest neighbour.

Sparsely along the creek, but ever thicker as the ground rose away from it to both sides, pine trees grew. Some of them grew from out of the lush grass, but others sprouted from the smallest crevices in rocks and outcroppings. They looked like climbers, clinging precariously to tiny footholds.

Spruce trees gave a bluish green cast to the higher slopes, towering over everything in majestic splendour. Across one of the distant hills the herd of wild horses was spread out, grazing. The great stallion stood apart, ever alert for danger to his harem. From this height and distance, they looked more like toys than real living creatures.

Jed picked a spot on the far side of the creek that was perfect for a building site. In his mind he built the house, the barn, the corrals. He pictured the valley dotted with cattle, wearing his brand. He saw himself astride a mighty stallion, with the stallion's harem now his own remuda. What a start this valley could give a man!

If he could just find a way to get a start! If he had just a few thousand dollars, he could multiply it many times over with a ranch like this valley would support.

Suddenly his life had a meaning and a purpose. When he was finished with this Avenger of Blood thing, he would return. He would homestead. He would begin a ranch. Maybe, just maybe, he had even found someone who would be interested in sharing his dream.

With difficulty, he forced his mind away from his dream, back to the present. Even when he had a job, he was a forty-a-month cowhand. There was little chance he would ever have such an opportunity. Some day, a foreman's job on a decent ranch, maybe. His own place was foolish to even think about.

After he had ridden the horse for nearly a week, he felt he was ready for the supreme test. He rode her close to the wild herd, using her to drive them further away. He wanted to do so for two reasons: he wanted to serve notice to the stallion that his mare was lost for good; he also wanted to be sure the mare was well enough under his control to mind his orders, even in the presence of the wild herd. She performed flawlessly. When the stallion came close to challenge them, he whirled a length of rope with a large knot in the end continuously. Whenever the stallion got too close, the whistling rope's stinging blows forced him to retreat. The mare never faltered. The stallion finally took his harem and fled.

Before the sun reappeared the next

morning he had the horse saddled, his things packed into his tightly tied bedroll and saddle-bags, and he began the long ride toward the Platte River.

The horse seemed to have forgotten her urge to run wild. She acted as though she had been his horse all her life. He rode into the fresh, new town of Douglas four days later.

9

Jed put his horse up in the livery barn, making sure to give her a generous portion of oats. He took time to get a room at the hotel, get a bath and a shave, and get a clean pair of pants and a shirt. It seemed like it was taking him forever! Then he almost ran across the street to Dr Ringer's office.

Della looked up from a desk where she was working on a large ledger. She beamed, leaped to her feet, and ran to him. 'Jed! Oh, Jed, I was so worried about you! I've found out a lot of things, and I wanted to tell you, and I was so afraid you'd get killed. You've been gone so long! Did you find Shaw? Was he alone? Are you all right? Where have you been? Oh, you look so good! But you've lost weight. Have you been hurt?'

'I ain't been asked that many

questions all at once since Pa couldn't find his chewin' tobacco,' Jed grinned.

Della stopped almost against him. She tipped her head back to gaze up into his face. It seemed the most natural thing in the world to put his arms around her. She responded instantly, putting her arms around him and holding him tightly.

He couldn't remember deciding to kiss her. If he had, the idea would probably have scared him so badly he might have run. He wasn't sure it was his idea, actually. One minute Della had her head against his chest hugging him. The next her head was tipped back, looking up at him. When he tipped his head down to look into her eyes, their lips were too conveniently close to stop and think about it. The next thing he knew their lips were together. His head started soaring. Sensations began surging through him that he sure hoped she wasn't aware of.

He stepped back and pushed his hat on to the back of his head. He felt as out of breath as if he'd run a mile or two. 'Wow!' he said. 'If I'd knowed kissin' a girl felt anythin' like that, I'da been doin' it a whole lot afore now.'

'You mean you've never kissed a girl before?' she teased.

He was serious at once. 'Oh, no, ma'am. I mean, Della. Can I call you Dell? Della sounds like a schoolmarm or somethin'. No, ma'am, I mean, Dell, I ain't never kissed nobody afore. Well, 'ceptin' my ma, when I was little. I ain't never wanted to especially, afore now. But I'd sure do it again, if you want.'

'You mean you've never even kissed one of those girls at the saloon?'

His face flamed. 'Oh, no! I never been like that there. I been brung up right.'

Her eyes danced and sparkled. 'Well in that case,' she said, 'you're probably right; you probably ought to have a little more practice.'

The idea sounded good to him. Real good. It was five minutes before he remembered something she had said.

'Hey,' he said, stepping back a pace, continuing to hold on to her hands. 'You said somethin' about wantin' to tell me somethin', or somethin'?'

She giggled. 'You really ought to learn to say *something*, instead of *somethin'* you know.'

'Huh?'

She giggled again. 'Never mind, silly. I did learn some things. I've had Father asking things of people, trying to learn something about Bart Shaw. He's a really bad man, Jed. He and three other men ride together a lot, and they're all really bad. They rob and kill for a living, and steal money or cattle and horses, but nobody's ever been able to prove anything to have them arrested. No woman is ever safe if they're around, especially if they're together. They are really awful, and I was so afraid they'd be together when you found him, and they would kill you. They've killed a lot of people.'

Jed felt as if time had suddenly been suspended. All sound disappeared except for some pulsing, rushing sound in his ears. He felt disconnected, somehow, from the whole world except for Della, standing before him. 'Three others?' he asked. 'Do you know their names?'

She nodded. 'Father found out a lot about them, really. Their names are Art Schnell, Billy O'Calloran and Frank Gates.'

Jed's face had gone deathly white. His voice, ringing with jubilance moments before, was suddenly so quiet it was almost a whisper. Almost without expression, he asked, 'Does he know what any of 'em look like?'

Della searched his eyes for a reason for the sudden change in his demeanour. She gripped the hands she still held, tightly. 'What's wrong, Jed? Yes, he got quite a little description. He said Art Schnell is a really big man. He wears some kind of miner's boots instead of riding boots, and always wears a bowler hat. You know, one of those little round things. And if

133

anybody says anything about it, or tries to make fun of him, he beats them up or kills them. And Billy O'Calloran is as little as Art Schnell is big. He's only about five-three, and has bright red hair. Somebody said he laughs a lot, but he gets really mad awfully quick. Nobody seemed to know anything special about Frank Gates. He's just always with the other three. That's all he could find out, so far. Why? What's the matter?'

Jed didn't hear her. He was looking at the dirt in a distant ranch yard. The mind of a tracker could always remember the details stamped in the dirt. That one scene especially was etched so deeply in his memory he could still look at it in his mind and pick out the tiniest of details. Some of the details of that scene he tried valiantly never to look at. It was the ground of that yard he was studying in his mind, remembering every mark.

He saw, again, the tracks of the big miner's boots. He saw the tracks of the riding boots so small they could have belonged to a woman. He saw the tracks of two men of ordinary size, unremarkable except for the left foot of one man turning in slightly. He thought the man might have had a broken leg at some time, and it didn't heal quite straight.

His voice was still that expressionless whisper. 'Did any of them have a limp, that anyone noticed?' he asked.

Della's eyes opened a little wider. 'Oh, yes. I had forgotten. That was the only thing anyone ever noticed about Frank Gates. He has something a little bit wrong with his left foot. It turns in a little, and he limps on that leg, but not very much. Why? Jed, I don't like it when you get like this! What are you thinking?'

The connection was too eerie to be coincidence. It fitted together much too neatly. After all these years he suddenly had names to put on four men who had done the unspeakable, the unthinkable, the unforgivable.

The eyes that looked at Della were suddenly flat, older, different. She almost shuddered as he spoke to her. The voice was still much too soft, but it was edged with brittle steel. 'Did he find out anything else about 'em?'

She shook her head, then her eyes flew open a little wider again. 'Oh, yes, he did. One other thing: somebody told him they liked to hang out at the One Mile Hog Ranch. You know, the one by old Fort Fetterman. Jed, what is it? What's wrong? I've never seen you like this.'

He looked at her, forcing himself from the cold loneliness of his reverie. He sighed heavily. ''Member, I tol' you 'bout my folks'n Bertie?' he asked softly.

'Yes. Why is that . . . ? Oh, Jed, they're not . . . '

He nodded. 'It's them. It's them, sure's Sunday. One of 'em was a big man in miner's boots. One was a real little man, track looked almost like a woman. One of 'em had a left foot that turned in, just a little. There was four of 'em.'

'Oh, Jed! Oh, dear. Jed, you didn't tell me whether you caught up with Shaw.'

He shook his head. 'I caught up with him, but he shot my horse out from under me. We was clear off back in the mountains. I hadta catch me a wild horse and bust her afore I could get back outa there.'

She stared at him incredulously. 'You caught a wild horse, on foot, without a horse of your own? You broke a wild horse to ride and rode out of the mountains on it? Jed O'Dell, are you stringing me?'

He grinned, relishing her amazement. The jubilance of his victory and his accomplishment eclipsed the sombre news she had shared. For a moment, he was himself again. 'Not a bit, little lady. This cowboy o' yours done just exactly that. It only took me less'n two weeks to catch 'er, gentle 'er down, bust 'er to ride, and make a real fine horse outa her. Why, she's so gentle by now you could hop on 'er an' ride 'er your own self. An' that ain't all, neither.'

Curiosity bubbled in her dancing eyes, in the tilt of her head. 'Oh? And what else are you about to surprise me with?'

He felt as if he were going to burst with enthusiasm. 'That valley up there, where I caught the horse, well, they's a whole herd of 'em. Gotta be more'n thirty. Good mares, and the finest stud horse you ever laid eyes on.'

'You're going back after him, aren't you?'

'Some day,' he nodded. 'But they's more to it. That valley is the most perfect spot in God's creation. It's got mountains up behind it, but it ain't up so high you couldn't winter right there. An' it's got water. A fine crick runs right down the whole length of it. An' the horses could make a man a start, and we could sell some of 'em as soon's I got 'em busted good, and buy cows, an' I got a little money saved up fer cows. It'd take another chunk o' money that we'd hafta figure out how to get from somewheres, but we could do it. An' — '

'We?'

'Huh?'

'You said, 'We could sell some . . . ' Who's *we*?'

Jed turned crimson. 'Well, I mean, uh, well, it was just sorta one o' them slips. I didn't mean, well, fact is, I been sorta thinkin'. Onct I get past this Avenger o' Blood thing, I was sorta hopin' maybe you'n me, that is I was sure hopin' a lot that you might be interested in teamin' up, and doin' that together. It's a plumb purty valley.'

'Why, Jed O'Dell! Whatever made you think I might be interested in doing something like that with you?'

He suddenly looked like she had kicked him in the stomach. She couldn't keep her face straight. She laughed brightly and put her arms around his neck. 'Did I hear a proposal in all that somewhere?'

'Nope.' Jed said instantly and firmly.

It was Della's turn to look stricken. Jed's eyes danced. 'But I'll tell you what. It ain't gonna be long afore I come a'askin', so you best get your best 'yes' all puckered up 'n ready.'

'What are you waiting for?' she teased.

Then the light mood was gone again, as quickly as it had come. An old familiar weight of necessity descended upon him, pushing him down, pressing him to action. 'You know I gotta go, don't you?'

Her eyes misted over. 'Where? Why?'

'I gotta find 'em,' he said. His voice was flat, quiet. 'I gotta find 'em, an' take care of it. I really am the Avenger of Blood for sure, now. I gotta go over to the Hog Ranch, and hang out till they show up. They'll come ridin' in, sooner or later. One at a time, or all together. It's somethin' I gotta do.'

'Oh, Jed! You don't have to . . . You could . . . Oh, Jed. You don't have to do that.'

'I got to. They ain't no other way. I got to, Dell. I'd rather stay here, with you, but I got to.'

'Oh, Jed! Oh, please don't let them kill you.'

'I don't aim to.'

She tilted her chin impertinently. 'And don't you forget what you're over there to do, Jed O'Dell!'

A sudden gleam momentarily relieved the flat hardness of his eyes. 'Now what would make me forget? The Hog Ranch is just a saloon. Oh, an' a dance hall. Oh, yeah, an' a whore house. That's all.'

'That's exactly what I mean, and you know it.' She grew suddenly serious again. 'Oh, Jed. Be careful. I want you to come back. Will you come back? To me?'

'I'll come back, if I have to crawl,' he said. 'I ain't never loved a woman afore. I ain't gonna stay away any longer'n I have to.'

She came into his arms again. Their lips met as though they belonged together. It was a kiss Jed would not quickly forget.

10

Death stared him in the face. It made him shiver in the unseasonable heat of the afternoon.

Jed looked over the place a long while before he rode on in. There was no sign of Shaw's horse. He put his own horse away in the barn provided. He couldn't shake the feeling that the hunted was watching him, the hunter, all the time. He was faced with a sudden conviction they would meet again in this hell-hole.

A lot of men had died in this place. Some of them needed to die; others didn't deserve to die, in such a place, in such a violent way. Some were just in the wrong place at the wrong time.

The One Mile Hog Ranch was a busy, bustling, boisterous place. The saloon building was fifty feet long and forty feet wide. The long bar allowed room for thirty or forty men to stand with one foot cocked on the brass rail. Close to a dozen tables were scattered about one side of the room, along the side and back wall. A stage graced the area fronted by a dance floor, clear of furniture. The stage itself was less than ten feet long. Two pianos sat on the dance floor one at each side of the stage.

'Two pi-annies in one place,' Jed marvelled.

Jed noted three doors leading out of the room, arranged along the back wall. Counting the front one he had entered, that made four entrances. One of the doors entered the lean-to that was the residence of Jack and Viola Sanders, who owned the establishment. There was a sign nailed to it that said, PRIVATE. KEEP OUT.

The other two doors led into the side of a long hall. One of those doors was close to each end. A door from the Sanders' quarters formed one end of the hall, an outside door formed the other.

Opening on to the hall from the back side were seven small rooms, where the working girls plied their trade. It was an assembly-line business, that only the loneliest of cowboys, miners or soldiers could have confused with romance.

Most of the men didn't care; they entertained no illusions of romance; they were just desperate for a woman. The Hog Ranch employed the worst, the oldest, the ugliest, the most diseased. It seemed to be no deterrent to the lonely that they would almost certainly take a case of 'drips' back home with them. For a few minutes, they had the exclusive company of a woman. It seemed worth the price.

The ceiling in the saloon and dance hall area was low. Twenty-five lamps hung from the walls. Between the lamps and the patrons vying to see which could produce the most smoke, a pall was supplied that hung thick in the air. In the centre of the main bar was a huge potbellied stove. The stovepipe extended straight up through the roof.

A dirty mirror graced nearly twelve feet of the back bar. Above it a large mural of a naked woman, lying on her side, offered tantalizing advertisement for the diversions available.

'Hi, honey! Wanta buy a lonely girl a drink?'

Jed stopped and stared at the woman who had greeted him. She couldn't have been more than twenty-five, but she looked tired and old, hard lines bracketing her mouth. Her smile was forced. Two teeth had been knocked out, or had fallen out. Her dress was cut provocatively low. He forced his eyes up to her face.

'Uh, no, I guess not, just now. Maybe later,' he stammered.

She laughed at his awkwardness. 'You have a drink or two, cowboy,' she said. 'The whiskey'll loosen you up some. I'll be back.'

She walked away with a swish of her hips. Jed swallowed hard. He laid a coin on the bar with his left hand. His right held his rifle. 'I'll just take a beer,' he told the bartender.

He carried the beer to a table along the side wall. He noticed another cowboy sitting two tables away, a beer sitting untouched in front of him. Something in his demeanour seemed singularly different from an ordinary cowboy. Jed couldn't put a finger on what it was. The man was staring at him. Jed nodded silently to the man, who returned the nod, then looked away.

Jed sat down with his back to the wall. He placed the rifle on the table in front of him, and felt, rather than saw, the other man watching him do so. He sat the beer between himself and the rifle and settled back to watch and wait.

It was only a little past the middle of the afternoon. He assumed the place would become increasingly active as the evening progressed. He had seen more activity at the building across the road as he had ridden in. He had taken time to check out that building as well. It turned out to be a dining-hall. A kitchen about five feet by ten feet occupied one end, the rest of the building was one long table, covered with a brightly coloured oil cloth. It would seat twenty people easily. For a quarter he was served a meal that was at least passable. Then he had come across the road to the saloon.

At the moment there were less than a dozen men in the place. Two girls whose clothing advertised their profession sipped drinks together at one table. The only girl actively working the sparse crowd was the one who had greeted Jed upon his arrival.

One of the men at the bar laughed suddenly, a little too loudly, at a story his companion was sharing. A cowhand crowded closer to get in on the amusement.

Four soldiers sat together at a table. They were having a lively discussion that, judging from their looks and gestures, involved one of the women at the other table. She gave no indication she was aware that she was the object of their conversation, or that she cared.

Three men were crowded around a roulette wheel located at the side of the dance floor. They were betting quietly, oblivious to all other activity. The place was quiet enough the dealer's voice, calling the numbers and the bets, and the ratcheting of the wheel as it revolved, were clearly audible.

As the afternoon wore on, the crowd slowly increased. Several more working girls came in from the back rooms and made themselves available to any patrons who might be interested.

A gambler, immaculately dressed in a broadcloth suit, came across from the hotel. He sized up the crowd, then began playing solitaire at a large round table. The nightly poker game would begin as soon as enough cowboys came in to get rid of their monthly pay.

A small, mousy man, his sleeves held up by elastic garters, sat down at one of the pianos and began playing softly. The three serious gamblers were still huddled at the roulette wheel, but the noise level no longer allowed the sounds of their effort to be heard.

Jed didn't realize he was staring at one of the girls. She bore some slight resemblance to Della. He was watching her but thinking of that certain doctor's daughter waiting for him in Douglas. Suddenly he saw her eyes go hard. Her mouth clamped to a thin line. Her face paled beneath the too-heavy make-up.

Snapping himself from his daydream, he noticed a marked stiffening in the attitudes of several of the girls. They were all staring at the front door.

Following the direction of their gaze, he belatedly noticed the group of men who had just arrived. They had walked in the door, then fanned out to study the interior. The man on the end to Jed's left was a big man. He stood six feet four. The small bowler hat he wore nearly brushed the low ceiling. He had a pair of shoulders that looked like he must have turned sideways to enter the front door. His feet sported black miner-style boots, planted in the sawdust of the floor as though grown there. His size made the tiny black bowler look almost comical, perched on top of his head.

The man beside him was nondescript. He looked tired, uninterested. He was average in size, in appearance, in build. He was the kind of man you could look at, look away, and forget instantly. There was nothing remarkable in his appearance whatever — except that his left foot was turned in, slightly.

The man next to him was quite the opposite. He commanded immediate attention. He was slight of build, finely featured, with a cocky grin gracing his face. His hands perched jauntily on his hips. Red hair curled out from under his hat. His freckled face made him look almost like a schoolboy. No hint of beard graced his jaw. His eyes danced with daring.

The fourth man was Bart Shaw, standing nearest the front door.

11

Jed felt the blood drain from his face. He licked his lips, but they still felt dry. His stomach knotted and he recognized the symptoms of raw fear. He looked again at the four men ranged along the front wall. He knew he could not stand against them. This was the hour of his death. For a moment he thought of quietly slipping out the back door.

Then his mind brought an unwanted parade of pictures before him again. He saw his mother and his sister lying in the yard. He saw the evidence of violent and wanton violation. He saw the holes between the eyes of each. He saw his father's crumpled, twisted body in the door of the barn.

His fear turned to ice, then melted away. All emotion drained from his mind. He slid silently out of his chair. He picked up his rifle, thumbing back the hammer. In the noise of the place, the click of the hammer cocking went unnoticed.

Jed walked slowly forward. He held the rifle at waist level, keeping it pointed at the middle of the big man's shirt. He was halfway across the room before the little man spotted him. He said something quietly, and the four men snapped their attention to him.

Others in the room noticed almost instantly. The evolving scene was all too familiar in this place. The noise level reduced as though someone were turning a concealed volume-control knob, until the room was utterly silent. The ratcheting of the roulette wheel was the last noise to stop, and it, too, fell silent.

'You danged idiot!' Shaw said with a curse of recognition. 'I should've finished you off when I shot your horse. How'd you get here?'

'That there wasn't too tough. I just caught a wild horse an' busted her. Then I rode 'er back,' Jed replied slowly. 'You're right: you should've killed me when you had the chance.'

'You still on that stupid mission, or whatever it is, for that girl you don't even know? What kind o' addled idiot are you?'

Jed shook his head. 'Not no more. That's what started me a-tailin' you. Not now. This is a whole lot more personal, now. I've waited five years.'

The men looked at each other, then back to Jed. 'Five years,' the big man rumbled. 'What you talkin' about?'

Jed took a deep breath. He did not allow the barrel of the rifle to waver. The silence around him made him feel as though he were in a huge cavern, where only he and these four men existed. 'Five years ago you four rode into a ranch yard up along Clear Crick. You raped and killed a woman and her daughter. The girl was just fifteen. Purty as a picture. You shot the man to pieces. They was my family. I am the Avenger of Blood. I come here to kill you all.'

The little man laughed suddenly. 'You, all by yourself, are going to kill all four of us? Us? Let's see you try it. You tighten that finger just a little on that trigger, and let's see how long you live. You ain't got a snowball's chance in hell against any one of us. There ain't nobody that stands a chance against the four of us. You're all by yourself, or did you forget that? Huh?'

'Not quite.'

The eyes of the four men jerked to focus on the man who had been sitting two tables away from Jed. He had walked, unnoticed, to a position about eight feet to Jed's right. His hand hung loosely, just above the worn handle of a Colt .45.

'Who are you?' the man who had to be Frank Gates asked.

'My name doesn't matter,' the man said softly. 'I am a range detective. I work for the Pinkerton Detective Agency. I have been hired to arrest the four of you for robbery and murder at Bridger's Crossing one year ago. Throw up your hands. You are under arrest.'

The small man cursed. That was the only clear memory Jed had of the events that followed. He knew the small man's hand streaked for his gun, but it was Frank Gates who was driven backward by a bullet to his chest. Then Billy took a bullet in his chest, still before his gun ever cleared the holster. Shots then were blasting and echoing with deafening confusion. The sound of the shots was mingled with yells and shouts and curses.

His first reaction was to squeeze the trigger on the rifle, still lined up with the front of the big man's shirt. He was aware the bullet drove the man back a step, but it did not stop his attempt to draw his own pistol. Jed frantically levered the rifle and fired again, then a third, then a fourth time.

At the fourth shot the man fell backward, crashing like a giant tree. Sawdust blossomed out around him as he landed. Jed had forgotten the existence of anyone or anything except the one man directly before him. He continued to stare fixedly at him. Suddenly it dawned on him there were three other outlaws.

Only then did he turn his attention to the others. Billy O'Calloran was lying on the floor, his head propped against the wall at an awkward angle. He appeared to have gotten his gun out of its holster before the stranger's third shot killed him.

Frank Gates looked as unassuming in death as he had in life, but he was the only one of the outlaws quick enough to have gotten off a shot. He lay crumpled on his stomach, curled to one side. His gun, too, was in his hand. A wisp of smoke still curled from the barrel. Bart Shaw was nowhere in sight.

The stranger stood with his .45 held loosely in his left hand. He was replacing the spent cartridges with his right. 'Thanks for taking the big man,' he said quietly. 'Four is a little more than I like to face at once.'

Jed was astonished at his casual

composure. 'Where's Shaw?' he asked.

'He dove out the front door as soon as the show opened,' the stranger replied. 'He rode off at a gallop, heading north-west, it sounded like.'

Jed looked back at the man he had shot. He lay without moving. His arms were spread straight out from his body. His feet were spread about two feet apart. His black bowler hat lay against the wall. His eyes stared upward sightlessly. Jed's stomach lurched suddenly. He clapped a hand to his mouth and raced out the front door. Outside he doubled over and retched violently. His knees felt wobbly; his head spun. He swallowed hard, wiping his mouth with the back of his hand.

'First one, huh?'

He turned and looked at the stranger. He was not a big man, but his chest and shoulders were massive. His legs looked almost comically short for his height. His face held no hint of mockery, only a quiet concern.

Jed nodded silently. The stranger

said, 'Well, if you're lucky, you won't have to do it again.'

Jed shook his head. 'Once more. I've still gotta get Shaw.'

'No. It's my job,' the man said quietly. 'I'll find him.'

Jed shook his head again. 'It's just a job, to you. I done been appointed the Avenger of Blood. It's my sacred duty. I gotta be the one to go after 'im.'

'Why?'

'That there's a long story.'

'I see no reason not to take time for a long story. There is no sense setting out after Shaw in the dark. Come inside and I'll buy you a beer, if you're a drinking man. You can tell me your story.'

'Uh, I don't drink. I just bought that one so's I wouldn't look funny sittin' in a saloon a'waitin. But I'd go fer a cup o' that coffee across the road at the chow hall.'

At the dining-hall they sat down across from each other on the long benches provided. There were only two chairs in the place, and they were marked with the names of Jack and Viola Sanders, the owners of the Hog Ranch.

After a few fits and starts, Jed told the story of his long quest to the quiet stranger. 'So you see, that's how come I got to be the one what goes after Shaw. I got to finish this.'

The stranger eyed him carefully. 'Can you?' he asked quietly.

Jed thought about it for a long moment. 'I can do it,' he said finally. 'I wasn't sure at all that I could shoot a man, till tonight. I'da just got myself kilt, if it wasn't fer you. You reckon Providence done sent you here to keep me from it?'

'I would not be surprised if that were the case,' the stranger replied.

'So you'll stay out of it? You'll let me be the one to finish this thing?'

The stranger studied him for a long, quiet moment. Finally he lifted his cup and drained the last of the coffee. 'Where will you come back to, when you've found him? Assuming that you survive.'

Jed answered with no hesitation. 'Douglas.'

The man nodded. 'I, too, have to see this through, but I have no deadline. I'll wait at Douglas for three weeks. If you have not returned by that time, I will have to resume the trail myself.'

'You talk like a schoolmarm,' Jed said suddenly.

The stranger just laughed. 'I have been well educated,' he conceded. 'One does not need be illiterate, you know. It pays great dividends to read and study all you have the chance. I was fortunate enough that my foster mother even taught me something of Latin and Greek. That's not as unusual as it may sound, though. Many of the men in this country are educated. I met a soldier with Custer's Seventh Cavalry a while back who used to be one of the Swiss Guard at the Vatican. It takes all kinds to make up a wild and free country like this.'

Jed nodded. 'My girl, she says she's gonna teach me readin' and writin' an' all that, after this here's over. Say, when you get to Douglas, would you tell 'er what's done gone on here? Tell 'er my folks is most all avenged, 'cept for just Shaw, and I'm gone off after him. Just tell 'er I'm still kickin'.'

'I would be most happy to,' the man agreed. 'Where will I find her?'

'She's Doc Ringer's daughter in Douglas. Her name's Della. Tell her, if, if I don't come back, tell 'er I love 'er, will ya?'

'I will tell her.'

Somehow that made Jed feel better as he rode out, at first light next morning. It still felt like he was riding the wrong direction, but what had to be done just had to be done. Even if he died in the doing of it.

12

Bart Shaw was really looking forward to the Hog Ranch. True, the food was middling at best and the beer, when they chanced to have beer, was pretty bad. The whiskey was even worse, but there were always the women.

He liked the whores at the Hog Ranch. It wasn't that they were pretty: there wasn't one in the bunch who could be called more than plain. Some of them were downright ugly. They were tired, old and well used. That was what he liked: he could do anything he wanted to them. He could abuse them as he saw fit. They deserved it, and they couldn't complain: that's what they were there for.

He thought of taking care of his horse, as they rode in together. He didn't intend to ride any more for a day or two. He'd need to put him up and feed him. Then he decided the horse could wait. It wouldn't hurt him any. He'd spent more'n one night tied up to a hitch rail in front of a saloon or a whore house. Eating post hay hadn't killed him yet.

He was the last one through the door into the saloon. It looked and smelled just the same as always: the same crowd, and the same ugly whores who invited abuse by their tired, worn and lazy efforts at satisfying men quickly. Well he didn't satisfy that quick. They'd earn their two bucks from him.

Then he felt the blood drain from his face. The noises in the One Mile Hog Ranch saloon faded to some place outside his awareness. He felt as if he were in a tiny bubble, suspended in the wrong reality. They were confronted by that starry-eyed idiot cowboy.

It was incredible! He was just a cowhand and scarcely more than a boy. How could he possibly cling to his trail so tenaciously? It was more incredible that he had been able to survive being left afoot in the mountains. The first thing he could think of to say was to ask how he had done so.

The story that he had caught a wild horse, on foot, broken it to ride, and ridden out of those mountains was too uncanny for even him to tolerate. Something in the way he held that rifle made him look different, older. More dangerous.

Then the second man bought into the confrontation. Bart recognized him at once. He had never seen him, but his description was known to every outlaw in Wyoming. He was a legend. It was said that you could hold a gun on this man, even a gun with a hair trigger, and he could draw his own gun and shoot you between the eyes before you could squeeze the trigger. He was reputed to be unbeatable in a fist fight, unshakable on a trail, and unerring in marksmanship. He could fight in ways people in this country had never even heard of, and you never knew if he was going to knock you out with a fist, a foot, or who knows what else.

In fact, the common wisdom was that if this man set out on your trail, the only chance of survival and freedom was heading for Mexico. Now here he was, facing them, declaring them under arrest for that episode at Bridger's Crossing.

Who would have thought anyone would still care about that? Who did they leave alive to tell who did it? Who would ever have dreamed someone would hire the Pinkerton agency to do something about it?

Bart licked his lips. He swallowed hard. He knew his only chance of survival was a well-timed exit through the front door. It was at his back, one step to his left. It was open to receive any slight breeze the unseasonable heat might allow. Just maybe, when the shooting started, he could get through it.

When he heard Billy curse, he knew the action was under way. Billy always swore just before he drew his gun.

Before the brash young outlaw had even finished the word, Bart lunged toward the door in a long dive. He landed on his shoulder, rolled to his feet, and lunged away again. He sprinted to his horse. Gunshots echoed behind him, giving him an adrenalin-induced burst of speed. Jerking the reins free of the hitch rail he vaulted into the saddle and jammed the spurs into the animal's sides.

The horse responded in pain and panic. Bart paid no attention to the direction the horse chose. He leaned forward, lying as flat as possible on to the horse's neck, in case any lead followed him from the saloon door. He kept jamming his spurs into his horse, in time with the horse's stride.

The horse laid his ears back against his head, stretched out his neck, and ran at his utmost speed into the gathering dusk. He ran flat out for a mile before Bart allowed him to slow down. He turned, then, to look for any indication of pursuit. He could see none. The horse was breathing hard and had to have a rest.

He reflected on the sounds that had followed him from the Hog Ranch. He clearly remembered at least four rifle shots. The young cowboy — what was his name? Jed, that was it. Jed something — he was the only one who had a rifle. He had been keeping it trained squarely on Art. Four shots. That meant Art was dead, for sure. He was positive the Pinkerton man would have killed Billy at once.

What was less certain was whether the Pinkerton man might have killed Frank, or Frank may have gotten him. Billy looked and acted the most dangerous. That was the mistake everybody always made. They somehow didn't pay any attention to Frank. Yet Frank was the fastest man with a gun among them, and by far the best shot. It was possible he might have gotten one or the other of the men who had confronted them.

He had heard a lot of shots. Four

shots by the rifle. Too many. That meant Frank had gone for the Pinkerton man. Then the kid with the rifle had either got Frank, or Frank was already dead. He wouldn't have had time to shoot the rifle four times if Frank had gotten the Pinkerton man first, then shot him. Frank was too fast, too good to allow that much time.

That meant he was the only one who had survived. I knew I had to get out of there, he congratulated himself.

Now what? That they would come after him, there was no doubt. Would they both come? That would depend on whether they had both survived, or whether either one had been wounded. He had to put some distance between himself and pursuit. He had to get some supplies and find out how many were trailing him, and who they were. Then he could decide what to do.

His horse had headed north-west from the Hog Ranch, and he had done nothing to change its direction. The Wind River Mountains lay in that direction. He had been there before. They contained myriad places a man could hide indefinitely. Of course, they also held the Shoshone Indians, but they were generally friendly.

As he rode, his fear began to subside. It was replaced for a little while by a feeling of invincibility. He was the only one who had survived. They couldn't kill Bart Shaw that easy. Then the feeling of exhilaration at his escaping unscathed began to fade. A growing anger began to take its place. It focused on the young cowboy who had pursued him so relentlessly.

'How can he just keep on comin' like that,' he asked his horse. 'How can he keep from gettin' killed, and just keep comin' and comin'?'

He wiped his mouth and nose with the sleeve of his long underwear. Then he used the same sleeve to wipe the sweat from his forehead. 'How can it stay this hot, this late in the year?' he asked peevishly.

The more he thought about it, the

more angry he became. By the time he decided to camp for the night, he had turned things in his mind completely. He was now the victim, relentlessly pursued and harassed by the merciless and dogged cowboy on some ridiculous mission of vengeance. He didn't have any business worrying about vengeance anyway: the one girl wasn't even any relation to him.

And he'd almost forgotten about that deal on the Little Thunder. They had had their fun, that day. He wanted to just ride on, but Billy wouldn't have it. He shot both of the women, and took a great delight in it. He shot the girl first, then the mother. He stuck his gun barrel right on the bridge of their noses, and squeezed the trigger. Then he laughed. Bart shuddered suddenly, remembering the kid's cold-blooded delight.

Who would have thought this persistent idiot would turn out to be part of the same family? Maybe the crazy cowboy did have some right to vengeance, but not against him. Against Billy maybe, but not against him. He'd just used the women the way women were meant to be used. He hadn't meant to kill them. It wasn't his fault at all.

The night was so hot and sultry he didn't even bother unrolling his bedroll. He hobbled his horse, used his saddle for a pillow, and dropped off to sleep.

He was up before sunrise. He built a small fire, made a pot of coffee, and ate a hurried breakfast. It was the very last of his supplies, and it left him less than satisfied. At least it was more than he would have had if he had bothered to take care of his horse before they went to the saloon at the Hog Ranch, he reflected.

He slopped the last of the coffee carelessly on his fire, and packed his things without bothering to wash them. Then he caught his horse, saddled up, and resumed his flight. He watered his horse and refilled his canteen at Willow Creek.

Near sundown he topped a hill above Brown's Spring and surveyed the homestead located there. Smoke drifted from the chimney. The two horses in the corral were old and bony, looking as though they would never live to see green grass. Oiled paper passed for windows in the front of the crude hut. Only the front needed windows. The rest was dugout, tunnelled back into the side of the hill. An old army blanket hung across the opening, serving as a door. It was so heavily soiled it was impossible to tell what colour it was supposed to be.

'Hardscrabble place fer sure,' Bart complained. 'Be lucky if they's enough supplies here to keep me goin' a week.'

He rode down into the yard. 'Hello, the house,' he called.

A hollow-cheeked homesteader brushed past the blanket in the doorway and blinked in the sunlight. 'Hello yourself,' he responded. 'Get down and come in.'

'Thanks,' Bart responded. 'Wouldn't have a bait of oats or somethin' for my horse, would ya? Been pushin' him pretty hard.'

'Ain't had no oats for my own horses all summer,' the man responded. 'They's good grass over along the crick, though. Let 'im eat a spell, while you come in an' fill your own belly. I was just whippin' up a little supper. Plenty fer two.'

'Thanks, I will,' Bart responded. He removed his horse's saddle and bridle, putting a pair of hobbles on his front feet. Then he led him over along the creek where the grass was best, and left him be.

He entered the homesteader's dugout. It reeked of grease and sweat and smoke, but he seemed not to notice. In spite of the bright sun, the lamp was lit on the table. It was needed, as the oiled paper let in very little light.

'Got some spuds a-fryin',' the homesteader said. He looked at Bart affably. 'Shot a prairie hen this mornin'. Biscuits is in the oven. I was just fixin' to make a bit o' gravy, when you rode up. Sit yourself down, and we'll fill our bellies good shortly.'

Bart sat down gratefully. The dugout did an excellent job of shielding the interior from the heat. They passed small talk until the meal was prepared. Predictably, most of the conversation centred on the unseasonably hot fall they were having. It should have frozen at least once by now, but the temperature still hovered in the nineties. When the meal was ready they ate in almost total silence.

The food was surprisingly delicious. Bart was ravenous from the exertion of his flight and scarce rations. Between them they ate every available bite, then used the last of the biscuits to wipe out the residue of gravy from the skillet.

The homesteader leaned back with obvious contentment. 'Best meal I've had in two weeks,' he complimented himself. 'Now if a man just had the makin's for a smoke, it'd be perfect.'

Bart pulled out a package of Bull

Durham and a packet of papers and tossed them to him. The homesteader yelped with delight and rolled himself a cigarette. He passed the tobacco and papers back to Bart.

The two sat and smoked in silence. Time began to nag at the corners of Bart's consciousness. He knew he couldn't waste any more time. He still didn't know how many, or who, were on his trail.

'I'm kinda short on supplies,' he lamented. 'You s'pose you could spare a few things to keep me eatin' till I have a chance to get to town? I'd pay you whatever's fair.'

The homesteader shook his head. 'Sure wisht I could,' he said. 'I ain't hardly got enough to get by on myself. If somethin' don't give purty quick, I'll be lucky to see green grass myself. I figger I'll likely have to eat my horses, afore spring.'

'It's a tough go out here all right,' Bart agreed. 'Still, I got some folks on my trail, and I ain't got too many choices. I'm just gonna have to have some o' your supplies. I wish I didn't have to take 'em, but I do.'

Realization dawned slowly on the homesteader that Bart was going to take what he wanted with or without his permission. He appeared to concede. 'Well, if that's the way of it, you'd just as well help yourself to what you want. I guess I can't stop you.'

With a move he hoped Bart would interpret as casual, he got up and flipped the butt of his cigarette out the door. Then he grabbed the rifle leaning beside the door and whirled toward the outlaw.

He was far too slow, too obvious, too clumsy in the attempt. Bart was standing with his gun drawn, waiting for the move he knew was coming. As the homesteader turned, he fired, driving the man out the door. He fired again, and the luckless homesteader dropped the rifle and fell backward. He twitched and jerked, moaning softly.

'Sorry to have to do that,' Bart said

with sincerity. 'It's just that I gotta have your stuff. At least it won't short you none. You won't be needin' none of it.'

The homesteader was still twitching and moaning as Bart rode out of the yard, thirty minutes later. He had found a disappointing amount of supplies, but enough to keep him going a couple weeks at least. It would have to do, for now. He'd find somebody else along the way to relieve of their supplies. There had always been more available when he had needed it.

Next he would have to find a convenient spot to watch his back trail. Then he could find out whether he was up against the Pinkerton man, the cowboy, or both. If it turned out to just be that meddling cowboy again, he'd finish him for sure this time. He'd had all he could stand of the man's inept but seemingly charmed stubbornness.

'I sure hope he's the only one coming,' he said. His voice shook with rage as he thought about the problems the man had caused him. 'He's one dead cowboy, if he is,' he assured himself. 'I'm gonna be sure he knows it's comin', an' I'm the one a'doin' it, an' I'm gonna gut-shoot 'im an' then watch 'im squirm. I'm gonna laugh at 'im, an' spit tobaccer juice in his face, an' tell 'im how much fun his little sister was, all the while he dies. I'm gonna get even with him fer ever' bit o' grief he's caused me.'

He crossed the open ground of a long, broad meadow, and entered the timber at the other end. Twenty yards inside the timber he found a spring, feeding a tiny rivulet of water. He stopped, looking around. He dismounted and walked back to the edge of the timber. 'This is just perfect,' he said with satisfaction. 'No matter how he tries to follow me across that open stretch, I can watch him from right here in the trees. I can move whatever way I need to, to be right there in front of him. Then, when he gets right up to me, I can step out and have him cold. He'll be in the wide open. He won't have no way to duck at all. If'n it's that Pinkerton guy, I'll just plug 'im from the trees. I ain't about to take no chances with him. I heard too many stories 'bout how good that man is. But if it's that cowboy, I'll let 'im sweat awhile, then I'm gonna gut-shoot 'im.'

He found a place well into the timber to picket his horse. He arranged his camp to wait as long as necessary. He fixed a place for his camp-fire where the glow could not be seen at night, and where the branches above would dissipate the smoke, making it invisible by day as well.

Then he took both pistol and rifle and positioned himself at the edge of the timber. He found a spot to make himself comfortable. He could see without being seen. All he had to do was wait.

If that idiot still wanted vengeance, he'd show him what vengeance felt like. Only Bart Shaw was going to be on the other end of it.

13

Riding toward almost certain death gives poor sleep. Jed was out of bed and gone with the first rays of sun. He headed out the same direction the outlaw had fled, confident he would not have to waste much time casting around for Shaw's tracks.

He knew Shaw was still riding the same horse he had been following so long. He knew the tracks of that horse as well as he knew his own face in a mirror.

He also knew he was no match for Shaw. If it came to any kind of showdown, he would be killed; if he gave the outlaw an even break, he would be killed; almost any way he could imagine the outcome, he would be killed. Still he had to go. He could no more refuse to finish what he had started than he could decide not to breathe. Better to die than to violate his sense of honour.

He found the trail almost at once, and set off to follow it at a ground-eating trot. He noted that the outlaw had ridden his horse at a dead run for more than a mile.

'Plumb scared, he was, Lucky Lucy,' he told the sorrel mare he had grown quickly fond of. 'It musta been that Pinkerton fella he was so scared of. He sure ain't never been scared o' me.'

That made him think again of the fascinating range detective. A sudden thought struck him. 'Hey, I wonder if he's the same Pinkerton guy what kilt them six Puckett boys, after they'd shot 'im an' he didn't have no gun, no more. I ain't never been sure I believed that story altogether. Still, if'n that was him, I can see why Shaw lit out 'steada stickin' around to fight 'im.'

At Willow Creek he found where Shaw had stopped for the night. He took advantage of the opportunity to fill himself and his horse with water, as well as his canteen. Weather this hot drained the moisture from man and beast at an alarming rate. Then he pressed on.

The sun was just kissing the tips of the Wind River Mountains to the west when he topped the hill and looked down on the homestead at Brown's Spring. The shadows were too long to be certain, but he thought he could see a shape lying partially outside the door of the shack. He pursed his lips thoughtfully.

He turned his horse and circled to arrive from the opposite side. As he did, he cut across the tracks of Shaw's horse, still bearing north-westerly. He pondered the fact for a moment, then continued his approach to the home-stead. On the hill above the dugout he dismounted. He drew his gun and cocked it. On foot, he crept forward until he could see down over the edge of the rude shelter.

The homesteader's feet were clearly

visible, toes downward, extending outside the door. They did not move. Studying the marks in the dirt, Jed could see where he had fallen. Blood on the ground indicated his wounds were severe and had bled profusely. The ground was scuffed and marked where he had twisted in pain for some time, then turned to crawl into the house.

Lived quite awhile afore he either passed out or died, Jed surmised.

He walked to one side and slid down the hill to the yard. He walked over and carefully checked the interior of the shack. It was dark and empty. He lowered the hammer on his Colt and holstered it. He knelt to examine the homesteader. He was dead.

He looked around the shack, noticing the obvious signs of hurried ransacking. 'Killed 'im, just so's he could take what supplies he needed,' he gritted.

Against his instincts, he took time to bury the homesteader. It sorta seemed fitting, when he had finished, to remove his hat and say a brief prayer for a man he had never known.

Then, because it was dark by the time he had that done, he decided it was as good a place as any to spend the night. He turned the homesteader's horses loose, so they would be able to survive. They headed for the creek at a fast trot and plunged their noses into the cold liquid. They had obviously been without a drink for a long while.

He picketed his own horse on a good patch of grass near the creek. Then he used the stove in the shack to fix himself some supper. He decided he'd rather sleep outside, however.

The next morning he waited eagerly for daylight. The air felt strange, and he wanted to see the sky. As the sun neared the eastern horizon, he began to understand the odd feel of the air. 'We's about to see this hot weather come to a real sudden end,' he muttered to his horse.

The sky in the north-east was black as coal against the horizon. The black clouds were fronted by towering dark clouds with white tips. Ragged tatters of cloud streaked like fine fringes from the towering masses.

'It's hotter'n blazes this mornin', but you're gonna be wishin' for a winter coat afore night, ol' Lucy,' he warned the horse again. 'We'd best be movin' quick, or we'll lose Shaw's trail in a whole bunch o' cold rain. Or worse.'

He saddled quickly. He helped himself to a few supplies Shaw had neglected to steal or ruin. 'Don't feel just right about that,' he told his patient horse, 'but that fella sure ain't gonna need 'em no more. At least he's buried proper. Maybe I shoulda made a marker fer 'im, but I ain't got no time.'

He rode out at a trot. The trail was easy to follow. So was the course of the towering cold front approaching from the north-east.

It was just past noon when he sat in the edge of the timber, watching a broad grassy valley. Shaw's tracks led straight across the middle of it. It was nearly half a mile, at the shortest point, to the timber on the other side.

'That there's a death trap, sure's sin,' he told his horse quietly. 'If he's a'lyin' up in the trees on the other side, he can pick me off like a rabbit afore I ever see 'im.'

He looked at the edges of the valley. Any direction he could circle, the clearing was blocked off by towering cliffs of reddish-grey rock. To circle the whole valley would take at least a full day. 'By the time I do that, that there storm's gonna be here, an' I'll never find the trail. Well, girl, I guess we's just gonna have to chance it. I sure hope he's still scared enough o' that Pinkerton fella that he just keeps on a'runnin'.'

He entered the open area slowly, his stomach cramped into a hard knot. He drew his rifle from the saddle scabbard and levered a shell into the barrel. That action cocked the hammer as well, and he left it cocked. He laid it across the saddle in front of him. He kept hold of the pistol grip. His finger stayed on the trigger.

Every step the horse took felt like it was carrying him to his doom. He moved forward steadily. Then he was within rifle range of the trees. He braced himself, watching feverishly for any sign of motion.

When he was within a hundred yards of the trees he thought he heard something. He jerked the rifle up, but saw nothing. He turned his horse sideways to the trees and studied them carefully, but could see nothing out of the ordinary. Nothing moved. No twig seemed out of place.

He placed the rifle back on the saddle in front of him and turned the horse toward the trees again. Now he was less than fifty yards from the cover of the timber. His heart pounded wildly, and he could hear the surge of his blood rushing in his ears.

He was less than ten yards from the nearest trees. His horse's ears shot forward and she shied sideways. He nearly lost his seat.

'Don't touch that rifle!'

His head snapped around. Twenty feet to his left Bart Shaw stood. He had stepped out from behind a tree, his pistol in his hand, pointing steadily at Jed.

'Get down off that horse, slow and easy. Hang on to the rifle by the end of the barrel.'

Jed looked around wildly, but he had no chance to run. There was nothing he could dive behind for cover. He was caught in the open.

He stepped down from the saddle. The thought ran through his mind, I ain't never gonna see Della no more. The memory of her fragrance slapped against his mind.

'Now lay the rifle on the ground an' step away from it.'

He did so: he had no choice. Watching Shaw, he knew beyond question he was taking his last breaths.

'What happened to Billy and Frank and Art back there?'

Shaw wanted to talk! He grasped at

the fact. At least that would let him live a few more minutes. 'They're dead.'

'What happened to the Pinkerton guy?'

'Nothin'. I talked 'im inta lettin' me come after you by myself.'

Shaw laughed coarsely. 'That had to be the dumbest o' all the dumb things you done,' he said. 'You wanta play hero and go for that gun now, or you want to just let me shoot you?'

'You can't just shoot me in cold blood!'

'Why can't I? I just point the gun at your gut, like this, so's you'll spend a lot o' time hurtin' an' cryin' afore you die. That's to pay you back fer all the miseries you caused me. Then I just squeeze the trigger, just like this.'

Jed watched in horror as the outlaw extended the hand, holding the unflinching pistol. It was pointed squarely at the middle of his stomach. He clearly saw his finger tighten on the trigger. He saw, as if it were all happening with incredible slowness, the hammer come forward. He saw the flash of fire from the sides of the gun's cylinder.

He braced for the impact of the bullet in his stomach. It didn't come. Then he realized the flash was too bright. The roar of the gun was all wrong. He focused his eyes on the end of the gun barrel. The slug was stopped, just barely protruding from the end of the barrel. Something was wrong with that cartridge!

Shaw realized it too, at the same instant. He looked stupidly at the end of his gun barrel and he knew immediately that he could not fire again. If he fired another shell, with that slug plugging the barrel, it would explode in his hand. He thought of his rifle, standing now behind the tree, nearly twenty feet away.

Jed clawed desperately for his gun. Shaw yelled and made a dive for the timber. Jed got his gun from the holster and fired wildly after the fleeing outlaw. Branches and leaves flew from all around him.

Jed scooped his rifle up from the ground and ran into the timber. Shaw's rifle was gone, grabbed as the outlaw fled past it. Jed could hear the sound of brush crashing. He fired his rifle in that general direction twice. He listened as the sounds of flight faded away. He holstered his pistol, then turned to get his horse.

Mounting, he took time to reload both pistol and rifle. Then he began following the trail of the fleeing outlaw, slowly and carefully. He worked his way off to the side of the trail, staying where he could clearly see it but not be within it, in case Shaw had stopped and waited for him.

He watched so hard his eyes ached. He watched ahead for any movement, any jay that scolded, any small animal frightened from hiding. It took a lot of time. He didn't mind. He had time. Five minutes ago he had thought his time had completely run out. Now he had lots of time. He was not about to hurry: he had no intention of walking into a second trap.

It was almost thirty minutes before he came to the site of the outlaw's camp. He saw the indications Shaw had saddled his horse and grabbed what supplies he could, and left at a run, through the timber. Abandoned supplies were strewn about the campsite. He followed, maintaining the caution that would, he hoped, let him keep living a while.

He shivered, realizing suddenly the temperature had dropped dramatically. He looked at the sky through the openings in the trees. It formed an unbroken black canopy above him. The wind, less noticeable in the trees, was picking up. The front had arrived.

Within an hour he had reached within his bedroll for a coat and put it on. Half an hour later he unrolled his slicker, and put it on over the top of the coat. He still felt cold. 'It can't possibly get that cold, that quick,' he complained.

Shaw's trail went crashing through whatever brush lay in his way, making no effort to find an easier path, fleeing in blind, frantic haste. Nevertheless, Jed stuck to his caution, watching carefully for any sign of trap or trick.

Within two hours there were flakes of snow in the air. 'Would you look at that, Lucy,' Jed muttered. 'It's been way too hot, way too long. I bet it was a hunert degrees yesterday. Last night it was so hot I couldn't hardly sleep. Now it's snowin'!'

Almost as though his words had triggered it, a wall of snow approached across a small clearing. He watched it in awe. Within minutes he was enveloped in a world of swirling, blinding, freezing white. The snow and wind were so thick and fierce he felt that he couldn't face it and breathe.

The trees at the other side of the clearing offered some protection. Within minutes, however, the branches were bowed under the weight of the heavy snow. Already Shaw's trail was solely visible by broken branches and trampled brush. There weren't even any hoofprints in the snow that was already covering the ground. Whatever tracks he left were completely concealed within minutes.

For a while, Jed tried to step up the pace. He had to stay close enough to see the trail. The weight of the sudden snow would soon be breaking branches, smashing brush, bowing trees so much the disturbance of Shaw's panicked flight would become indistinguishable. If he got far enough behind to allow the snow to completely hide that trail, he would have no way of knowing what direction Shaw went. Then he would be back in that position of not knowing whether he were the hunter or the hunted.

Within another hour he realized it was more important to find a place to weather the storm. The temperature continued to drop, swiftly and steadily. His breath made a frozen plume in front of his face. His toes already felt numb in his boots.

A big rock overhang appeared, facing the southwest. It offered some protection from the wind and snow. He rode into its shelter and dismounted. Working quickly, he cut several small pine trees. He dragged them to the protected spot and leaned them at an angle against the overhang. Then he led his horse into the relative shelter created by the overhang and the cut trees.

He hurried to find a supply of firewood, laying it just outside the shelter where it would be readily accessible. It took another hour of working feverishly to tighten the shelter and start a fire. He unsaddled his horse. There was scarcely room enough in the space for both of them, but he knew they had to stay close together to survive. He had weathered blizzards before, but he had never seen a storm begin so abruptly, or with such intensity.

By the time he had finished and built

his fire, the furious snow had already formed an unbroken canopy, clinging to the branches of the small trees he had leaned above him. The heat of the ground and rock made an isolated pocket of warmth in a swirling, frigid blizzard. Within that small circle it was surprisingly cosy.

Jed's horse reached out and nibbled the snow that sagged down inside the branches of their shelter. Once she got hold of one of the branches, and when she pulled on it, a cascade of snow showered them. She shook her head and snorted her disgust, then went back to nibbling snow for water.

Jed reached outside the end of the shelter and scooped up handfuls of the new-fallen snow. He melted it over the small fire, drinking some of it while it was still cold. Then he made coffee and ate some supper. He sat a long time, watching with amazement as the snow piled up unbelievably in the fading light. When it was dark, he wrapped up in his blankets and huddled against the face of the still-warm rocks and dozed. He woke to feed the fire from time to time. There was no sign of the storm lessening.

14

Dust hung in the quiet air. A mule deer nibbled leaves from a bush. She was unaware leaves shouldn't have been on that bush this late in the season. They should have been frozen off a month ago, at this altitude. By September, she should have been pawing the ground for dried grass, not browsing on still-green leaves.

She didn't mind. She'd had twin fawns that year, and the demand of their suckling had taken a heavy toll on her body. The late autumn had given her the opportunity to restore her body fat and she had used the chance well. She had far more fat along her back and around her middle than normal. She would winter well.

The freeze that nearly always triggers the start of the fall rut had not come this year. Does were coming into heat erratically, confusing the bucks. She was only just now beginning the first period of oestrus she had experienced this year, but had no way of knowing she would be better off if she remained unbred. If she were bred now, her next spring's fawn would be born late. Both hiding and nursing a fawn always took a heavy toll on her body. If it were twins again, that toll would be even heavier. She would have no time to recover from that toll before the following winter arrived. If it were a hard or early winter, she would probably not survive. The unexpected boon of this late autumn might well end up sounding the death knell for the graceful creature.

Other creatures of the Bighorn Mountains were experiencing similar confusion of their routine. All life in this harsh country moved in predictable cycles of heat and cold, plenty and paucity, life and death. When the cycles changed, or were unduly delayed, it was all thrown out of harmony. None of them understood that fact. Every level of life only drank in the unseasonable heat, enjoyed the unaccustomed ease, and reached out for the unusually plentiful food.

It was that way as well for the huge diamondback rattlesnake. The sun lay deliciously warm on his back. His reptilian mind was incapable of even wondering why it was still so warm. If he were blessed with such a mind, he might have understood the respite it gave. He might have understood how different it was from what the weather should have been, this late in the year. He might have understood the perils that respite would eventually bring. He didn't. All he knew was it felt good; it warmed his blood; it wakened his hunger; it gave him energy.

His tongue flicked in and out of his mouth continually, sensing the air for any hint of prey. Suddenly a tension rippled through his body. The keen sense of that tongue, constantly testing the air, detected a mouse. He tested the air again and again. It was approaching, drawing nearer, its scent steadily growing stronger.

He lay without moving. His body was stretched on the rock in a serpentine series of curves. From close to the ground he looked like he was just part of the rock. That position would allow him to strike just as well as if he had been coiled. His tail lay with its rattles silent on the stone. The only movement was the constant, almost hypnotic pattern of that forked tongue, flicking outward, sensing the air, retreating to the triangular-shaped head, flicking outward again in a rhythmic pattern. Out and back. Out and back. Out and back. Never moving. Always sensing. Out and back the tongue continued.

His tiny black eyes never blinked. The only movement he betrayed was the tiny darts of tongue that smelled the air with uncanny accuracy. He sensed, rather than saw the mouse as it scurried along seeking the food that would produce milk for its own young. The mouse had a litter to feed. Something in the air had triggered a primordial urge to fill her stomach, to store up an extra measure of nourishment against some impending need. Her constant need for forage was made more urgent than normal by that urge, reducing her level of vigilance.

She approached the rock, and stopped to nibble on a seed that had dropped from a yucca. She started on. She was almost within range of the snake's strike and needed only to advance another foot. The rattler's muscles poised and tightened. Then the mouse turned and darted two feet to its right. She grabbed a dead grasshopper, and lay down to eat.

She nibbled tiny bites of the insect until it was totally devoured, then snuffled the ground where the insect had lain. Then she turned again, scurrying toward the waiting serpent. The snake still did not move. He waited with infinite patience, the constantly flicking tongue sampling the air, tasting the rodent's nearness. Out and back the ceaseless tongue moved. Out and back. Out and back.

The mouse moved her front feet up on to the rock. She stayed there, standing on her back legs, sniffing the air. Her tiny black nose twitched and wiggled. Then she scratched and clawed her way on to the rock's warm surface. As she scuttled across a corner of the snake's rock, the rattler's head shot forward with blinding speed. Gaping jaws closed over the neck of the small animal. Hypodermic fangs injected venom into the rodent before her senses fully recognized her peril.

The snake retained his grip as the mouse squealed and struggled frantically to escape. She had only a rodent's mind and never thought of the litter of red-skinned, tiny young, squirming in a hidden nest. She gave no thought to the starvation and death they would endure within a day. She had no last vision of things that might have been in her rodent life: she was filled with nothing but that primitive, frantic urge to escape. Then even that began to dim and fade away. It took less than thirty seconds for the deadly venom to paralyse her heart. Consciousness gave way to encroaching blackness. Sensation faded. Her struggles ceased.

The snake did not loose its grip. Holding the animal firmly, fangs still deeply embedded, he began to move. He made a strange spectacle, head erect, holding the form of the dead mouse. His body moved, as if by some hidden engine, propelling him forward. The erect section of body topped by that head just moved straight forward.

Somewhere in his reptilian mind the image of a deep dark hole at the rear of a shallow cave called to him. It carried the memory of security and warmth. The mouth of that cave yawned in the wall of the canyon. It was nearly 200 yards away.

It was not a cavern, or even a very deep cave, it was more like a hollow that had been washed out by some ancient deluge. It had been worn steadily deeper, over countless years by people and animals seeking any kind of shelter. Parts of it bore the mark of tools that had been deliberately used to deepen it. Here and there one could see odd markings scratched into the rock. They looked like a child's stick drawings.

At the rear of the shallow cave a three inch crack in the rock gaped. The foot-high crevice opened into blackness beyond. Only the diamondback rattlers saw any welcome in that narrow fissure. To them it beckoned with all the attraction of home. To them it recalled memories of writhing, twisting masses of serpents, entwined together in ancient rituals of courtship and survival.

That defile opened into a larger chamber behind the rock. It had no other outlet. It had housed a den of their kind for countless seasons of hibernation and breeding. Even now, half a hundred of the poisonous creatures used it as a haven. Even though the weather was stiflingly hot, it was time to move to a place of hibernation, and they had responded.

That timeless call of hibernation was stirring in the huge snake's soul as well. Conflicting with that urge was an equally urgent compulsion to find seclusion to ingest his meal. He had no means to reduce the animal to bite-sized pieces. He had to eat it whole. To do that he must unhinge his jaws, then work the rodent, head first, down his throat, inch by laborious inch. It was a process that took time and presented special peril. During the time the animal was in his jaw, he could not defend himself. It would take a couple hours at best.

As he moved toward the distant cave with his prey, he passed the end of a fallen tree. Its trunk, slightly over a foot in diameter, was hollow in the centre. Disease or insects had eaten the life from the core of the tree, bringing its demise. Already eaten away from within, the dead trunk had been an easy victim of some great storm. It lay now in the dry October grass. Its dark and empty core was too great a temptation. The snake moved into its welcome gloom. He positioned himself carefully, where he could watch the only entrance to his retreat. He began the process of devouring the mouse's body that would provide him with nourishment through his hibernation.

The snake had no instinct that would lead it to watch the sky, no understanding of fast-moving cold fronts. He had no premonition of the sudden and severe change the weather was about to take. He only knew he had a meal, he had a place of seclusion, and he used it well.

He finished the taxing chore of ingesting his meal. It was a good meal. She was an unusually large old mouse which would carry him through the winter's hibernation comfortably and well. Filled and content with the surfeit of flesh slowly digesting within him, he lay unaware of the temperature's sudden drop. The fast-moving front swept down from the frigid north-east. It began to rain, but the rain changed to snow within an hour. The wind howled, dropping the temperature almost seventy degrees by morning.

By the time the snake sensed the change in climate, his body was far too cold and lethargic to respond to its desire to seek the warmth of the underground den. The snake, like all of his kind, was a cold-blooded creature with no mechanism to maintain body temperature which took on the temperature of his surroundings. His blood thickened; his senses dulled; his body lost all sensation.

He would live again, when his blood warmed sufficiently, if he didn't freeze solid. Even then he might live again if he didn't get broken or discovered and eaten by some scavenger first. But for now he was only a helpless and harmless form.

As he lost all sensation, he remained oblivious to the role destiny had slated him to play.

15

Bart Shaw pulled his hat down tight against his upturned collar and shivered. It was not only the cold that caused the tremor; it was just as much a shudder of fear and incomprehension. He felt pursued by demons he could neither fathom nor escape.

The force of the driving snow was impossible to face and breathe. Cold seeped in through gloves and coat and chilled his bones. He had to find shelter quickly, or Jed would find only his frozen form. If Jed survived. It had to be just as cold for him. But Jed was different: his life was charmed; he couldn't be killed. Even when he had Jed dead to rights, something happened. Now even his .45 was useless. He'd have to take it apart and find a strong stick of hardwood, smaller than the barrel. Then he could use it to drive that slug from the barrel. He had to do that before he could use it again.

What was there about Jed O'Dell that made him such an unstoppable nemesis? Why did he have all the good luck, while, he, Bart Shaw, had all the bad luck? It just wasn't fair. It wasn't reasonable. It wasn't even sensible.

He slapped his thighs to try to stimulate circulation, but couldn't even feel the blows. 'I got to find some place to build a fire,' he said for the tenth time.

Maybe it was destiny for him simply to die in the storm. He knew only too well the deadly toll Wyoming winters took on lives of people and livestock. He personally had known half a dozen men who had frozen to death, even though they were dressed and prepared for the onslaught of winter. He was neither prepared nor dressed for it.

A brief respite in the relentless wind brought a glimpse of a dark shape against the canyon wall. His head snapped up. His heart stopped for an instant, then began to beat frantically. He turned his horse toward it, forcing the animal to lunge through the deeper snow that lay in the partial shelter of the wind.

'A cave!' he breathed. 'It's a cave! Maybe it's my turn to have some luck, for a change. I may live to tell about this yet.'

He approached the gaping hole in the canyon wall carefully. It was nearly eight feet high, but went less than fifteen feet into the side of the mountain. Places on the walls looked like they bore the marks of tools, but he couldn't be sure in the dim light. Strange scratchings marked one wall of the rock.

'It's good enough,' he told his horse. 'If I can get a fire started at the mouth o' that cave, we'll be plumb warm. It's only just turned cold. The rocks is still warm. It won't be hard to heat it up.'

He dismounted and led his horse into the shelter. The animal blew appreciatively. The sudden respite from the frigid wind was so welcome, Bart had to force himself back out into it to hunt for wood. The walls of the cave still emanated heat, but he knew it wouldn't last long.

'Gonna be next to impossible to find wood under all this snow,' he muttered.

He kicked along through the snow, picking up every stick of any size his feet encountered. He made four trips back to the cave with kindling, but he knew he wasn't finding enough wood to last out a blizzard of this magnitude.

As he started back out for the fifth foray, he stumbled across a fallen tree, buried in the snow. He stopped and kicked snow away from it. It was a whole tree, a little over a foot in diameter at the base, that had been toppled by some storm. It would be fairly dry beneath its fresh covering of snow. The storm was so sudden the moisture couldn't have soaked very far into the wood. He studied the problem a long moment, then turned back to the cave.

Picking up his horse's dragging reins, he spoke. 'C'mon, horse. You're gonna drag that there tree in here. I can burn it for three days, if I have to.'

The animal was less than enthusiastic about going out in the howling cold again, but he dutifully responded to the insistent jerking on the reins and cursing of his master.

Bart worked the end of his rope under the trunk of the tree, then tied a slip knot in it. Then he dallied the other end around his saddle horn and led the horse back toward the cave. The rope tightened. The horse strained forward. The rope hummed with the wind blowing across its tension. The horse leaned into the task, feet slipping on the snow. Suddenly the fallen tree began to move.

As it moved, it began to shake loose its burden of snow. Each loss of weight made it easier to move. It also began to slide up on to the top of the snow. The horse was able to pull it with relative ease by the time they got back to the cave. Bart shortened the rope and kept the animal working until he had the base of the tree right where he wanted to build his fire. Only then did he allow the animal to retreat to its better shelter at the back of the cave.

He worked slowly and clumsily as he arranged wood next to the end of the dead tree. He cut shavings from the driest piece of wood. They peeled off dry and thin, excellent for kindling a fire.

When he had it as receptive to fire as he could manage, he withdrew a packet of matches wrapped in oilskin. Striking one, he sheltered it carefully from the random gusts of wind that found their way into his shelter. With care and great patience he managed to nurse a tiny flame to life in the pile of shavings.

He carefully added shavings and sticks to the infant flame until it gained enough strength to dry and ignite the larger pieces of wood. Bart heaved a great sigh of relief when he realized he had fire enough to depend on. He was going to survive! No stupid curse was strong enough to beat him. He was a survivor! He'd live to spit on the dead, frozen body of the inept idiot he could not seem to kill, whose pursuit he could not shake.

He removed the saddle-bags from behind his saddle and began to arrange things to make himself some coffee and a meal. As an afterthought, he removed the saddle and bridle from his horse, replacing them with a pair of hobbles in case the storm subsided and the animal wandered outside while he slept.

He arranged the burning wood so the end of the tree would be more fully in the flames. 'Probably have to saddle that horse up again every time I need to pull the tree in further,' he muttered. 'Shoulda just left it on 'im. I will next time. Let 'im wear it. Ain't gonna kill 'im.'

He settled back against the wall of the shallow cave and sighed contentedly. He was going to win! In a minute, he'd fix some supper. He'd have a cup of coffee, while Jed froze to death, out there in the storm somewhere. He chuckled.

Inside the log, the heat of the fire warmed the interior of the hollow space. The blood of the lethargic rattlesnake warmed and thinned. He began to stir, moving first this way, then that. Heat continued to build. Smoke began to fill the air of his narrow prison. Its acrid bite assailed his eyes and nose. The smell awoke an instinctive fear deep within him. He moved more quickly, feeling a swiftly rising tide of agitation. He kept trying to move away from the heat and smoke, but his way was blocked by the end of the hollow section. His only escape lay directly toward the oppressive heat.

Bart stirred himself from his rest against the wall of the cave. He chuckled again as he looked at the ferocity of the blizzard raging beyond the fire's glow. 'Freeze, you dumb nuisance!' he yelled out into the night.

He rummaged in his things and

brought out a coffee pot. He stepped to the mouth of the cave and reached out, scooping it full of snow. He set it on the fire to melt. He decided to move some kindling further into the hollow log, to ensure its becoming dry and hot before it needed to burn. He arranged sticks carefully, reaching back and forth across the burning hollow end of the dead tree.

Inside that tree, heat continued to build. The reptile slithered as close to the light flooding in from the open entrance as he could tolerate. Shadows moved back and forth, raising the level of his fear and wrath. His tail vibrated his rattles furiously, but the sound was lost in the crackle of the flames. Then a hand came into view at the end of his fiery prison, arranging a burning firebrand.

The serpent's reaction was instantaneous and fierce. His head shot out from the end of the burning log and fastened on the hand. His fangs shot venom with all the ferocity of his anger and discomfort.

'What? Hey! Aaaah!' Bart yelled, leaping back.

The snake clung tightly, dangling from his extended hand. As he tried to shake the thing from him, it loosed its grip only long enough to bite again.

A rattlesnake can make venom as rapidly as a person can gather saliva in the mouth, so the next bite had just as much poison to inject as the first.

Bart kept yelling as he shook his left hand violently. His right hand pulled his gun from his holster and he pointed it at the deadly serpent. Then he remembered he dared not fire it. He dropped it in the dirt.

He grabbed for his rifle, trying to find a way to kill his attacker. Finally, when the rattler had bitten him twice more, he shook it loose. He fired at it, missing its head but striking it about halfway along its body. As it writhed and thrashed, he fired twice more before he finally got a bullet into its head.

Suddenly the horse broke past him.

With his front feet hobbled, he had to leap with both front feet together, then bring both hind feet forward to lunge again. Hobbles were nothing new to the animal, though. He was filled with a mindless terror by the sound of the snake's rattles, then the gunshots in so closely confined a space. He lunged across the fallen log, scattering the fire, and disappeared from view almost immediately.

Even in death the large snake kept writhing on the ground. Cursing, Bart kicked it into what was left of the fire, past the coffee pot that had already spilled its contents, putting out most of the flame. He threw his rifle into the dirt. Moving with great haste he pulled off his coat and shirt, then jerked back the sleeve of his long underwear. He looked stupidly at the four sets of twin punctures in his skin.

'What am I gonna do with that?' he asked.

Bart cursed again. He cursed his horse. He cursed the snake. He cursed the blizzard. He cursed Jed O'Dell, who was out there somewhere in the darkness, stalking, always stalking.

'What is there about that man? Why won't he leave me alone?'

A sudden inspiration lightened his face. 'Tobacco! Tobacco's a good poultice. I'll put tobacco on 'em. That'll draw the poison out. I'll still get sick, but I'll live.'

He pulled out his brick of chewing tobacco and bit off as large a quid as he could fit into his mouth. Heart pounding, he chewed as fast as he could. His jaws hurt and ached, but he dared not slow or stop.

He chewed until his jaws would no longer obey. Then he plastered the tobacco on to two of the bites. He broke off another chunk of the brick. His jaws hurt. It didn't matter. He had to keep chewing: his life depended on it.

It seemed to take forever to get the second batch chewed up. By the time he thought it well enough pulverized and moist, his vision was blurring. His heart was racing far too fast as he plastered the juicy brown glob of tobacco on the last of the bites. He leaned against the side of the cave.

'Gotta move the wood a little,' he said, slurring the words. 'Gotta stoke the fire up. Hey, the fire's out! Horse musta scattered it too much. Stupid animal! Just like 'im to run out on me just 'cause he got scared. I'll shoot 'im when I find 'im. That'll teach 'im. Better get the fire goin' again. Gettin' colder in here. I'll rest just a minute first. Just a minute. It hurts. It hurts so bad. I ain't never had nothin' hurt this bad.'

16

Sometime in the grey hours of morning the wind and snow began to subside. Jed stayed where he was, the unaccustomed cold seeping into his bones. He continued to feed the fire. Water dripped from the branches of the trees he had leaned against the rocky overhang. It formed pools that his horse stooped to drink, from time to time.

Melting some of the nearby snow, as he had the night before, Jed made a pot of coffee and ate breakfast. He put on all the clothes he had with him against the bitter cold. He thought it had to be close to zero; it might even be ten below. He had leather gloves, but only unlined, working gloves. He had nothing to keep his hands warm in weather this cold.

'Sure wish I had them big ol' mittens I got me last winter,' he told his horse.

'I'll hafta find me another pair o' them. They sure was warm.'

By shortly after what he thought must be noon, he decided the storm was about over. By mid afternoon he was in the saddle, following his instinct of the way the fugitive had been fleeing. He made slow progress, allowing his horse to pick the easiest route around and through the drifts of snow.

The air was sharp, clear and unbelievably cold. The sky was brilliant crystalline blue. No more snow appeared imminent. A coyote raised his head and studied him. He stood there, his face covered with snow from seeking a mouse he sensed beneath it. He merely watched Jed's passing as though knowing the man meant him no harm this day. An eagle circled in the sky, seeking one last meal here. Nightfall would find him shifting his hunting grounds to the friendlier weather and lower elevations.

Suddenly Jed jerked his horse to a stop. A tiny wisp of smoke had caught his eye before it vanished into the clear air. He studied the area where he had seen it, but saw nothing more. He knew he had seen something, though. His eyes were sharp from too many years in the open. A cowhand has to see what's there, and make accurate snap decisions based on those glimpses, or he will not long survive. Jed never considered doubting what he had seen.

Touching his horse cautiously, he urged the animal on along the floor of the canyon. Less than a hundred yards later he halted the animal again. 'Saw it again, Lucy,' he told his mount. 'Keep your eyes open.'

Emerging from a patch of aspens, he spotted the dark semicircle against the wall of the canyon. His hand slid out of his pocket. He pulled off his right glove and drew his .45. He shook his head, he replaced the pistol and drew his rifle instead. He levered a shell into the chamber, cocked it, and laid it across the saddle in front of him. He put the glove back on. 'Fingers is gonna get too stiff to pull the trigger, if'n I don't,' he muttered.

Even through the glove, the harsh cold of the rifle's steel stung his hand. He urged the horse forward. As though sensing her master's caution, the big mare moved slowly, silently, picking her steps carefully through the knee-deep snow. They moved over to the same side of the canyon as the small cave. Jed dismounted. Moving stealthily, he approached the cave from against the canyon wall, where the drifting snow had left a foot-wide path almost bare.

He stopped just beside the mouth of the cave and listened. There was no sound. He leaned outward enough to see the fire Bart had built at the mouth of the shelter. Only the tree trunk showed any sign of remaining fire. An occasional tiny wisp of smoke wafted from one small spot near its base. The rest was cold, dead ashes.

Jed looked around him carefully. Couldn'ta lit out yet, he reasoned. There'd be tracks. Looks like his horse mighta lit out last night, though. That might be tracks of a hobbled horse runnin' under the last few inches of snow.

He leaned his head into the cave mouth and jerked it back quickly. The motion drew no fire from within. He analysed the picture that instant glance had given him. His movement was too quick to be certain, but he thought he had seen Bart, leaning against the wall of the cave. The position, the attitude of the image that had impressed itself on his mind seemed, somehow, all wrong. He looked again.

This time he left his head exposed for an instant longer. The picture was much clearer, even in the contrasting dimness of the shallow cave. He frowned in confusion. He looked again, once more jerking his head back quickly. Then he stepped into the open, rifle held at waist level, pointing at the figure of the fugitive.

Bart didn't move. His eyes still seemed to burn with hatred. They bored into Jed. Jed moved to one side, but the eyes did not follow him. They remained fixed, unseeing, unfocused. Bart's left arm was extended almost horizontally from his shoulder, bare of clothing, horribly discoloured, grotesquely swollen. He was frozen into that position, still sitting against the wall of the cave.

Jed walked carefully into the cave. He waited for his eyes to adjust to the gloom. He nudged the frozen body of Shaw. 'Froze plumb solid,' he mused. 'Look at that there arm! I ain't never seen nothin' look like that afore. You 'spect maybe that's gangrene? What would he get gangrene from?'

He looked around the cave carefully. Finally he spotted the scorched remains of a large diamondback rattlesnake. It lay at the edge of the fire, that had obviously been scattered by something. Bart's rifle lay in the dirt to the right of the dead fugitive. Jed's lips pursed thoughtfully as he holstered his gun and studied the cave's interior.

That arm's been snake-bit! he realized suddenly. There musta been a rattler in here. I wonder if it was in the wood? Maybe it got caught in that dead tree when this here cold snap hit.

He walked over and studied the base of the hollow tree. 'I bet that's it!' he said. 'I betcha anythin' he was right inside there! I betcha the fire warmed him up. It woulda made him plumb mad, too. Then, when Shaw let his hand get too close to the end o' that holler tree, he struck it. Prob'ly whilst he was a'feedin' the fire. Looks like he managed to shoot 'im. I bet he plumb panicked his horse doin' it, though.'

He laughed suddenly. 'That woulda been somethin' to see! That poor horse! It musta been scarier'n anythin' he'd ever seed. The snake a'rattlin', Bart a'yellin', gun a'shootin', the fire makin' spooky shadows all over, and thet poor horse trapped agin' the back o' the cave. It'll prob'ly take me three days to find 'im and two more to get 'im settled down enough to load Bart's body on 'im for the trip back.'

It didn't matter. Bart wasn't going anywhere. The cave was as good a place as any to make camp. He'd find the horse today, then start back to Douglas tomorrow. He might move Bart's body outside for the night, though. He'd stay, frozen solid.

He suddenly felt a heavy, unexpected sense of having been cheated. He'd been so certain his duty and his destiny had been to bring the man to justice. Then he had found Bart was part of the group who had murdered his own family and that cemented the conviction. It was his solemn and sacred duty to bring this man to justice, kill him, or die in the attempt. He had decided there really was something to this Avenger of Blood thing.

He had been faithful to the mission he thought was his. Even when he had been convinced it would only lead to his death, he had not abandoned the chase. He had done his best. He admitted it was a stumbling, bumbling best at times, but it was his best. He deserved to be able to complete his mission.

Instead it was a nearly mindless reptile whose destiny had been to bring about that justice. His mother's voice spoke out suddenly in his mind. ' "Vengeance is mine, I will repay, saith the Lord".'

Jed repeated the words aloud, softly. 'I remember Ma sayin' it. Many's the time I heard 'er say it.'

He rebuilt the fire as he thought about it. When it was flaming brightly he made himself a pot of coffee. Then he sat down, his back against the rock, and framed another question. 'Does that mean I wasn't the Avenger of Blood at all? Or does that mean I done my part, an' the rest got took care of, fer me? Is that there how come Shaw couldn't never kill me, even though he was lots better at killin' folks? Was this here some accident, or was this here the way it was supposed to be?'

He'd ask Della about that, as soon as

he got back to Douglas. He had no way of knowing, of course, what was waiting for him. He had no knowledge of the rewards paid for the three outlaws killed at the One Mile Hog Ranch. The Pinkerton detective had disdained any of that money, and had given it to Della to save for Jed.

He had no way of knowing the reward outstanding on Shaw as well. When he returned the body to Douglas he would be a rich man with more than enough money to start that ranch he had dreamed about. He just didn't know it.

If he had known, he probably still wouldn't have thought much about it. He was too busy thinking about Della. He would learn the rest soon enough.

THE END

We do hope that you have enjoyed reading this large print book.

Did you know that all of our titles are available for purchase?

We publish a wide range of high quality large print books including:
**Romances, Mysteries, Classics
General Fiction
Non Fiction and Westerns**

Special interest titles available in large print are:
**The Little Oxford Dictionary
Music Book, Song Book
Hymn Book, Service Book**

Also available from us courtesy of Oxford University Press:
**Young Readers' Dictionary
(large print edition)
Young Readers' Thesaurus
(large print edition)**

For further information or a free brochure, please contact us at:
**Ulverscroft Large Print Books Ltd.,
The Green, Bradgate Road, Anstey,
Leicester, LE7 7FU, England.
Tel:** (00 44) **0116 236 4325**
Fax: (00 44) **0116 234 0205**

*Other titles in the
Linford Western Library:*

STONE MOUNTAIN

Concho Bradley

The stage robbery had been accomplished by an old woman. Twine Fourch had never heard of a female being a highway robber before. He followed the trail all the way to a dilapidated log cabin up Stone Mountain. What happened after that no one could believe even after townsmen from Jefferson found the old log house and the skeletal dying old woman. But before the mystery could be solved there would be two unnecessary killings, a bizarre suicide and a lynching.